Crystals and Conspiracies

Beth Dolgner

Crystals and Conspiracies
Crones of a Feather Paranormal Cozy Mysteries, Book Four

Ebook ISBN-13: 978-1-958587-46-1
Print ISBN-13: 978-1-958587-47-8

Published by Redglare Press

Cover Design: Melody Simmons

https://bethdolgner.com

CONTENTS

CHAPTER ONE

"THAT *IS* MY PIN!" With a huff, I entered the four-digit code on the keypad again.

The ATM made a loud beep, and a message popped up on the screen. *Incorrect PIN. Please try again.*

"I know my own PIN!" Yes, I was talking back to a machine. Briefly, I glanced around to see if anyone was witnessing my increasingly embarrassing attempt to withdraw cash. Luckily for me, it was early in the morning, and no one else was at the bank yet. My black 1978 Cadillac hearse was the only car in the parking lot.

The wind whipped against my cheeks, and I could feel them becoming numb. I hadn't bothered to button my coat or put on my knit cap before jumping out to get cash, even though the ATM kiosk was outside, near the front door of the bank.

The entire point of these machines was that they were quick and easy.

Or, at any rate, they were supposed to be.

I could feel my magic building up in sync with my increasing aggravation. Later, once I was inside the hearse with the heater cranked, I could do a brief shedding spell to rid myself of the excess magic. At the moment, though, I wanted my money.

In my mind, I pictured punching in the four-digit number on a keypad. It was the same PIN I'd had since I opened the account at the bank there in Foxfire Haven, Washington, when I'd returned last summer.

It was now early March, and I was certain I hadn't suddenly forgotten the code I'd been using for nearly nine months.

I took a deep breath and pressed a finger against the *two* button. "I know my own code, you stupid, stubborn machine!"

I selected the next two numbers slowly, so I wouldn't have any doubt I had gotten the number correct.

Then, I pressed the last number. "Give me my money!" I commanded the ATM as I jammed my index finger against the *nine* button.

There was a loud crackling sound as a white arc of electricity shot out from the spot where my fingertip and the button met. The shock rocketed through my finger and up my arm as I jerked backward with a yelp.

This time, the ATM did not inform me I'd gotten the wrong number. Unfortunately, it didn't give me the money I was trying to withdraw, either. Instead, the screen fizzled out.

It was dead.

I stared at the machine while I absently sucked on my injured finger. It stung from the electric current that had shot through it.

Did the machine zap me, or did I zap it?

There was no way to know, but I suspected I was the one to blame.

Or, rather, my magic was.

I pressed my face into my hands. "I don't understand," I moaned. I had returned to my magical hometown to get my power under control. At first, it seemed to be working. I was getting better at recognizing when I had an excess of magic, and I knew how to quickly and safely slough it off.

Lately, though, I'd been having more uncontrolled outbursts of magic. It was almost always when my emotions were heightened. Anger, fear, and frustration were the biggest culprits. My magic would increase so quickly I wouldn't even realize it had happened, and it would burst out of me in a puff of sparkly pink ether. If it was a small outburst, it was at best a little funny and at worst embarrassing. The big exhalations of magic, however, could be dangerous.

And, now, I could add "ATM killer" to my list of magical calamities.

Since the bank hadn't yet opened for the day, there was no one I could report the broken ATM to. Later, after the first delivery on my schedule, I would either call or stop by the bank again. It would be embarrassing to admit what I'd done, but I knew it was the right thing to do.

I trudged to the hearse, turned on the engine, and cranked the heat as high as it would go. While I thawed out, I thought back over the most recent magical exhalations I'd had. I always thought of them as magical farts, but they were becoming more like magical explosions.

I'd sent a supernatural shockwave through my subdivision two weeks before, and it had rattled the windows of one house so much that the owner had called the

Foxfire Haven Constables, certain something suspicious was going on.

Chief Constable Wyatt Hightower had been at my front door five minutes after receiving the call, asking me what I'd done this time. Since he lived just a few doors down from the former funeral home I lived in, his own windows had rattled, too, and he'd known immediately it had been my fault.

That incident had been both dangerous and embarrassing, the worst combination possible.

My cheeks were gaining feeling again, and the sting in my finger was fading, so I decided to hit the road. I felt like I was fleeing the scene of a crime, even though I didn't have any money in hand to show for it.

I eased the hearse onto the two-lane road leading away from downtown Foxfire Haven and in the direction of the next town south of there. Calling Brentwood a town was generous, since it was really just a crossroads with a general store, a cafe, and a gas station. A few houses were tucked away in the forest nearby, and that was it.

Still, the cafe in Brentwood apparently had biscuits so good that some of the people in Foxfire Haven swore the owner must be a witch, even though he seemed oblivious to the supernatural world. A natural witch, some called him, born with an inherent magic that required no knowledge of potions, spells, or any other aspect of witchcraft.

Brentwood Bites was in the same building as the gas station, and the wooden structure looked like it might fall down at any minute. The faded-green paint was peeling, and in several places, loose boards dangled by only one or two nails, threatening to fall right off the side of the building. Despite the building's raggedy appearance, and the town's tiny size, at least ten cars were already parked in front of the cafe.

I found the owner, Mike, at work behind the counter inside. He had a sheen of sweat on his forehead, but he was also grinning as he pulled a sheet pan out of the oven. The smell of cinnamon rolls permeated the crowded cafe.

"Hi, ma'am, what can I get for you?" Mike asked me after he had safely placed the rolls on a countertop. He wiped his flour-covered hands on his black apron, which was covered in just as much, if not more, flour.

"I'm Hazel Underwood from Dead Easy Delivery. I'm here to pick up the biscuit order for the Foxfire Haven Rotary Club."

Mike's face lit up. "Right, the lady with the hearse! Give me two minutes!" Mike disappeared through a swinging door behind the counter, and while he was gone, I shut my eyes and enjoyed the feeling of the cafe. People were chatting happily, the smells were comforting and homey, and the quiet tinkle of forks on plates seemed almost musical.

Marlee would love it here, I thought. As an empath, she would enjoy soaking up all the good feelings inside the cafe.

True to his word, Mike was back in a couple of minutes. He had two white pastry boxes in his hands, and as he passed them to me over the top of the counter, he leaned forward and cocked an eyebrow. "I hear Foxfire Haven is into magic and stuff. Like, witchcraft and everything."

I opened my mouth but paused, trying to choose my words carefully. The supernatural world was a closely guarded secret, despite the fact we existed side-by-side with the non-magical world. Finally, I grinned wickedly at Mike. "And I've heard the same thing about you." I tapped a finger against the top of a box. "Word has it these biscuits are magical!"

"That they are." Mike leaned even farther over the top of the counter, like he was about to reveal a big secret. "And there are two extra in there for you, so you can taste the magic for yourself."

I thanked Mike at least three times before I finally left.

Once I had delivered the biscuits to the community center, where the Rotary Club was meeting that morning, I headed home. I didn't have another delivery scheduled until eleven o'clock that morning, so I had time for a luxurious breakfast of biscuits and strawberry jam.

The old funeral home had belonged to my uncle Grant, and I had been surprised to learn I had inherited it from him after he died. I had been even more surprised to find I really loved living there, in part because I had three roommates who had become both my friends and my coven. Marlee Yamada, Jo Davenport, and Valerian Bellamy helped breathe new life into the funeral home, and I was so grateful to have their support as I tried to get my magic under control.

Since I'd be heading out again soon, I drove the hearse up the circular driveway in front of the sprawling one-story brick building and parked in front of the porch steps. There was no reason to squeeze into the garage out back, since I'd be leaving again in a couple of hours.

I walked into the house quietly because I expected Valerian would still be asleep. I didn't know when she had gotten home from her shift at Sit a Spell Tavern the night before, since I'd gone to bed before she arrived. In the kitchen, though, I found Jo and Marlee already up. They were both sitting at the small table in the breakfast nook, drinking coffee under the watchful eyes of their familiars. Stella, a glossy black toucan, was perched on the table next to Marlee's elbow. Jo's pelican, Gordon, had settled onto a spot on the floor that was directly in front of the radiator.

"You had an early morning," Jo said in greeting.

"But it was worth it, because I came back with biscuits. I'm willing to share." I had wrapped up my two biscuits in a napkin before dropping off the rest to the Rotary Club. As I put the bundle on the countertop, I heard a low coo from Perkins, my burrowing owl. He lifted his tiny head expectantly from his flannel-lined nest near the radiator. "No biscuits for the familiars! I was talking about sharing with Jo and Marlee."

Perkins gazed at me coolly through half-closed lids. Even at his diminutive size, he still had the owl glare down pat.

I divided up the biscuits, grabbed the butter and jam from the fridge, and settled in at the table with Jo and Marlee. I had only taken one bite when my cell phone rang. I swallowed hastily and answered it.

"Hazel?" I immediately recognized the voice as belonging to the owner of Stacy's Stationery and Sundries. "I need help! My self-warming teacups are on the fritz, and we have to isolate them! Can you please help me get them to my storage unit?"

I had no idea what "on the fritz" could mean when it came to teacups that had been spelled to keep their contents warm, but I was already jumping out of my chair as I promised Stacy I would be right there.

I shouted an explanation to Jo and Marlee, who wished me luck before I hurried out of the house and into the hearse. Stacy's shop was in downtown Foxfire Haven, and it only took a few minutes to drive there.

When I pulled up in front of her shop, everything looked fine. I got a spot on the curb, so we could easily move the rogue teacups from the shop to the back of the hearse.

When I walked inside, though, things were not fine, at all. The teacups had been arranged on a shelving unit, and Stacy often filled some of the cups with water to demonstrate their magic. Except, at the moment, the teacups were overheating the water, and steam was rising from them. Some were even boiling over, and water was running down onto the floor. A smaller bookcase nearby had been splashed with water, and the display of stationery there had turned into a soggy pile of lavender-colored paper. Every single teacup was vibrating, and the rattling sound echoed in the small store.

"They're overheating!" Stacy shouted when she spotted me in the doorway. Her fingers were pink from the scalding water. "I can't stop them!"

In my surprise and panic, my magic spiked. Before I could do anything, it shot out of me in a gale-force pink wave that pummeled the teacups. Stacy was knocked backward by the force as every single teacup shattered.

Chapter Two

The crash of teacups gave way to the sound of the last shards tinkling onto the shelves and the floor below. The whole mess was covered in a hazy layer of my magic, and the pink shimmer seemed garish in the overhead lights.

Stacy made a small noise of disbelief, and I looked over to see her leaning heavily against the side of the checkout counter.

"Are you okay?" I asked quickly.

After a few moments of silence, Stacy nodded. "I think so. But my teacups!"

I felt tears welling up in my eyes. "I'm so sorry. I am so, so sorry, Stacy. I will help you clean this mess up, and then I'll pay for all the teacups and any damage I caused."

It's going to take a lot of deliveries to make up for this expense.

My heart sank. Dead Easy Delivery had become a success, and I used a lot of the income from deliveries to pay for repairs to the funeral home. Between deliveries and the rent money I got from my roommates, I had been able to make a lot of significant repairs and upgrades to the place. Until I paid for all these teacups, though, any further improvements would have to wait.

"I'll get the broom and the mop." Stacy gazed mournfully at the remains of her teacup display. "And the trash can."

As she turned and shuffled toward the back room with slumped shoulders, another realization hit me. If word about this got out, it would damage my reputation. Business owners in town might not want to trust their goods to a witch whose magic was out of control.

And, in a town as small as Foxfire Haven, it was very likely that news about my latest magical explosion would be part of the gossip circuit by dinnertime.

When Stacy returned, I took the broom from her and began to sweep up the mess. No, not the mess. *My* mess. I wanted to apologize, again and again, but I remained quiet. I would do that later, once Stacy had recovered from her shock and disappointment a bit. First, we had work to do.

Porcelain shards had skittered halfway across the shop, and it took a while to get everything collected and thrown into the trash can. Once I was finally done with the sweeping, Stacy began to mop up the water.

That part, at least, hadn't entirely been my fault. The teacups had been overflowing before I arrived. It was a small comfort, but comfort, nonetheless.

After a few silent minutes, while I continued to look for stray shards and Stacy mopped, she sighed heavily. "Tenth grade, at the antique mall in Stanton."

"I'm sorry?"

"Tenth grade," Stacy repeated. She propped the mop against the counter and gestured toward the display that had once housed the teacups. "I had a magical outburst while my mom and I were browsing the antique mall in

Stanton. She was looking for some vintage dishes, and I finally admitted to her that I was on the verge of failing math class. By the time I'd gotten the courage to tell her, my magic had built up, and it just"—Stacy curled her hands into fists, then opened her hands and spread her fingers wide—"flew out of my body. I destroyed seven antique lamps, and we had to make up a story for the owner of the store."

I nodded in understanding. Stanton was a non-magical town, and a magical exhalation like Stacy had experienced would be hard to pass off as a simple accident. "What's been happening with my magic, it does remind me of how it was for all of us during our early teen years," I said.

Stacy gave a short laugh. "Non-magical people think puberty is so awful, but at least they get to avoid the spikes of magic. That stuff always worked its way out at the worst possible time."

"Always," I agreed.

"Anyway, I'll accept your help paying for the teacups, but you'll only be paying my cost, not the actual price tag. Plus, I'm going to call my supplier and have a chat with him. If the cups hadn't gone haywire in the first place, they wouldn't be broken now. I'm guessing I can get at least a partial refund."

"Thank you." I felt a tightness in my chest loosen slightly. "And I promise to do a shedding spell before any future visits to your store."

Stacy gave me a sharp look, and the tightness returned as I braced myself for a lecture. Instead, what she said was, "Don't be so hard on yourself. You once told me you didn't practice magic for twenty years, and it's going to take time to get back in the habit again. This rough period won't last forever."

"Thank you," I said again. I didn't mention the fact that my magic seemed to be getting harder to control the longer I was in Foxfire Haven. Instead, I told Stacy to let me know what I owed her once she did her tally, then said goodbye.

When I slid behind the wheel of the hearse, my phone buzzed to alert me to a new text. It was from Jo.

I wrote an intention to have a quiet day at work, it read. *When I got to the office, I found out our editor and half the staff had called out sick.* The message was followed by an emoji of a sad face.

Jo's manifesting magic was strong, but it had a tendency to backfire, like getting the quiet workday she wanted only because the newspaper staff had been hit by a wave of illness.

I texted back that my magic was causing problems, too, with a promise to explain that evening. By the time I got home, there was another text from Jo waiting for me, declaring that we should share details with each other over dinner at the tavern.

That sounded like a great idea to me, and it gave me something to look forward to as I made my eleven o'clock delivery, which was quick and uneventful. It also gave me the extra courage I needed to call the bank, though that went better than expected. Apparently, blowing up the ATM was a relatively common occurrence, and the bank's on-call electrician had already fixed it.

Valerian came into the kitchen shortly before lunch. "I'm too good for my own good," she said, then yawned widely.

"Busy night?" I was unloading the dishwasher, and I paused to glance at Valerian. Her long white hair was loose instead of in its usual braid, and she had yet to change out of her red flannel pajamas.

"I'm glad my latest potions are popular, but we're getting bigger crowds at the tavern, and they're staying later than usual." Valerian pulled the coffee pot off the burner, then frowned when she realized it was empty.

"I prepped it for you, but I didn't know when you'd be getting up," I explained. "Just flip the switch, and you'll have coffee in no time."

Valerian did as instructed while I continued, "Your boss should give you a commission on every sale. Your potions are making him a lot of money!"

Despite Valerian not being quite awake yet, her face broke into a wide smile. "I'm making a lot of money, too! Tips have been great."

Not only was Valerian good at potions, but she also made great cocktails. By combining the two talents, she was keeping customers at Sit a Spell Tavern happy, and she was coming home with wads of cash tips.

"Jo and I will see you tonight," I told her. "We're meeting at the tavern for dinner, and I'm going to see if Marlee wants to join us."

Valerian looked around. "Where is Marlee, anyway?"

"Working on her massive to-do list. Remember, she's got three spring weddings coming up, plus a bunch of other events."

"Well, I don't have to be at the tavern until four o'clock this afternoon, so my current to-do list consists of drinking coffee, taking a leisurely shower, and doing a little online shopping with my extra tip money."

I slid a few plates into their spot inside the cabinet. "Sounds divine." I would tell Valerian about my teacup misadventure that night, I decided, when I was sharing it with Marlee and Jo, too. There was no need to spoil her current mood.

My two afternoon deliveries didn't involve anything breakable, but just in case, I performed a spell to shed any excess magic before both of them. Only a bit of magic puffed out both times, and since there were no dishes going rogue at either client's location, the deliveries were made without a hitch.

I got home with just enough time to park the hearse and walk to the tavern. Physical activity was always a good way to keep magic in balance, and although the weather was cold, it wasn't raining, and it felt good to be outside as the last bit of daylight slowly faded from the sky.

The brisk air helped clear my mind and lift my spirits, and by the time I reached the front door of Sit A Spell Tavern, I was ready for dinner with my coven and, perhaps, even a laugh over my incident at Stacy's shop.

Well, maybe I wasn't quite ready to laugh about it yet.

The squat, half-timber building that the tavern called home always made me feel like I was walking into the Middle Ages, and with the nearly dark sky and the cold air, the warm golden light that spilled out of the front door as someone walked inside felt particularly magical.

The magic faded as soon as I stepped over the threshold. The crowd was larger than usual, as I had expected, and there was a cluster of women huddled together near the front door. One of them was somehow making her body so wide that I couldn't get past her. She was holding her arms out to her sides, one palm facing up and the other hand holding onto a wine glass that was in danger of sloshing its contents over the rim.

"I'm not kidding!" said the woman in a shrill voice. "I haven't cursed anyone since a bad breakup in college, but if she doesn't make things right, I will put a curse on her that will make her wish she'd agreed to refund my money."

The woman was tall, with a wide nest of teased brown hair that fell to her shoulders. Every time I tried to move around her, she would shift enough that I was still stuck with my back against the door.

"Surely you can get Adeline to apologize," said one of the other women in the group. All four of them standing there looked to be around my own age of fifty-three, and the three faces I could see were all frowning.

"Yeah! It's her fault your spell backfired so badly," another woman said. "You could also pursue legal action."

I stopped trying to get past Ms. Big Hair and began listening. The only Adeline I knew of was Adeline Beaumont, the owner of Into the Cauldron. Adeline—who wasn't a witch but a vampire, despite owning the town's magic store—didn't like me one bit. I wondered why the witch threatening to curse Adeline blamed her for a spell gone wrong. Had Adeline sold her the wrong items for a spell, or had the items been faulty somehow?

I thought of the teacups, remembering that even tried-and-true spells could go awry if a magical element wasn't quite right.

"Hmph." The woman in front of me crossed her arms, giving me just enough space to squeeze by her. As I went, I heard her say, "Casting a curse would be a lot more fun than suing her."

I spotted Jo and Marlee already seated at the bar on the far side of the tavern, and Jo's hand rested on an empty stool they were saving for me. The women by the door were likely a coven, and I said a silent thank you that my own coven was so much warmer and happier.

I took exactly three steps when I felt a strange prickle against my arms. "Oh, no," I muttered. "Not here. Not now."

Except, it wasn't my magic causing the feeling. I could tell it wasn't at a critical level, and there was no telltale pink puff around me. I glanced around, wondering why I was feeling so strange, and locked eyes with a man who had a square jaw, long dark hair, and a burning hatred in his dark eyes.

And he was staring directly at me.

He's not glaring at me, I realized. *I'm just in the way.*

I turned around and found myself face-to-face with a blond man who was exactly my height. His intense gray eyes stood out in his pale face as he stared in the direction of the dark-haired man. When his lips pulled back, I caught a glimpse of fangs.

I had just walked between a vampire and his enemy.

Chapter Three

I DARTED OUT OF the path of the gray-eyed vampire, sidestepping so I was no longer caught in the staring contest happening between him and the dark-haired man. Immediately, the tingle I had felt on my skin disappeared, but I could still sense the heaviness of the atmosphere.

"I knew I would find you here," the vampire said.

"Because you're in my territory," the other man spat back. "Which, as you should remember, you promised to steer clear of."

"And, as you should remember, I told you I don't honor any territorial claims by werewolves."

When the argument had begun, most people in the tavern were still going about their business, chatting happily and sipping their drinks. At that pronouncement by the vampire, though, a hush fell over the room.

I had met several shifters, but I had never heard any of them talk about territories. I even recalled some of the things I had learned about werewolves in school, and one of the facts that had stuck in my mind was that, sometime in the early Victorian era, werewolf packs had made peace with each other, and territorial disputes had come to an end.

And I had never heard of a turf war between vampires and werewolves. It sounded so cliché, like something out of a bad horror movie or a supernatural remake of *West Side Story*.

The werewolf slowly rose from his stool. As he sauntered toward the vampire, everyone in the vicinity moved backward. There was the grating noise of chair legs scooting across the wooden floor, and those of us who were standing took a few steps back.

"What do you want, Vincent?" The werewolf stopped a few paces away, and it was clear that he was much taller than the vampire. Taller, but not necessarily more powerful. Both werewolves and vampires were incredibly strong.

"I want you and yours to stop spreading rumors about me. I've lost half my clients because of your lies."

The werewolf shrugged. "What makes you think I've been wasting my time talking about you?"

Vincent sneered. "Because every time a client tells me they're taking their business elsewhere, the Ulmann name comes up. They ran into you at the store, or their kids were talking to your kids at school. Don't play dumb, Connor. It doesn't suit you."

Connor rolled his shoulders back and crossed his muscular arms over his chest. "And if my family has been telling the truth about your unsavory practices, what are you going to do about it?"

Vincent stepped forward, the hint of a wry smile on his lips. "You can't bully me."

"Bet I can." Connor's arms unfolded in a flash, and his right fist shot forward.

It wasn't fast enough for a vampire's reflexes, though. Vincent simply leaned to one side, and Connor's punch struck nothing but air. Connor bent at the waist and charged Vincent, but again, he failed to make contact. Instead, Connor hurtled into a group sitting at a small round table behind Vincent. Several drinks went flying, and a man was knocked out of his chair as Connor sprawled on top of him.

"Enough!" I heard Valerian shouting from somewhere behind me.

Over that, a male voice shouted, "Break it up!" I assumed that was Will, the owner of the tavern.

Neither Vincent nor Connor listened. Even as Connor was picking himself up after crashing into the table, Vincent made his first strike. He darted forward and snapped an elbow up, catching Connor's jaw. The force of the hit sent Connor stumbling backward, and he nearly fell onto the table again.

"Take it outside, now!" It was definitely Will doing the shouting, because he appeared at the edge of the circle we had all formed around the scene. His face was red with anger, and while I didn't know what kind of supernatural creature he was, he looked like he was ready to take on both the werewolf and the vampire single-handedly.

Vincent glanced at Will, which gave Connor the advantage he needed to land a punch. Vincent reeled, but soon, he was in a fighting stance again.

Before he could retaliate, though, a voice boomed, "I don't think you heard Will." My chest felt like it was reverberating from the deep voice, the same way I had once felt the loud bass in my chest at a rock concert.

Across from where I was standing, I saw the fur-covered head and shoulders of Barry, Foxfire Haven's resident Bigfoot and a regular patron of the tavern. He had just walked inside, and he strode toward Vincent and Connor as people deftly dove out of his way.

Barry didn't stop moving until he was directly between the vampire and the werewolf. "Which one do you want me to escort outside?" he asked Will.

"The wolf," Will answered as he stepped up and curled a hand around Vincent's upper arm. "Let's go, vamp." As he led Vincent toward the back door, I heard Will say, "I don't care what you do outside of this tavern, but in here, we do not fight."

Connor tried to resist, backing away from Barry and claiming he had every right to sit and drink a beer in peace. Barry, undaunted, closed the space between the two of them until his honey-colored fur was nearly brushing Connor's nose. Connor was tall, but even he had to crane his neck up to look Barry in the eyes.

"Fine," Connor muttered. He turned and stalked toward the front door, and Barry stayed close behind.

Slowly, people began returning to their conversations, and I knew they were all discussing what had just happened. I made my way to the stool Jo and Marlee were saving for me, so we could do our part in supporting town gossip.

"Since when are vampires and werewolves in some kind of territorial dispute?" Jo asked in greeting. The fingers of one hand were wrapped around several of her long black braids, a nervous habit of hers. The purple streaks in her hair were hardly visible in the tavern's dim lighting.

"And what was Vincent doing that was so, to quote Connor, 'unsavory'?" Marlee was turned around on her stool, still facing the direction of the confrontation between the two. "What a strange situation."

Valerian appeared on the opposite side of the bar. She had a glass in one hand that she was expertly adding various liquids to. "Connor is in here pretty often, but I've never heard him talk about a territory before. I know there are some old grudges between the two supernatural camps, but I didn't think any of those rivalries existed in Foxfire Haven."

Marlee ran her palms along her glossy black hair, which was pulled back into its usual low ponytail. Then, she gave herself a shake. "Yuck! Both of them were so angry. I understand Vincent being mad if Connor is spreading rumors about him, but I wonder what made Connor do that in the first place?"

"Apparently, this unsavory business of Vincent's," I said.

"Alleged unsavory business," Jo pointed out. "If the two of them dislike each other, who knows what lies either one of them has said about the other?" She drew in a deep breath, then let it out in a loud sigh. "But it's not our business! Tonight, the only business we have is eating tasty food!"

Marlee shook her arms, flinging little bits of dark red magic from her fingertips. The magic drifted to the floor harmlessly, and it would dissipate in just a few minutes. As an empath, she had literally felt the same feelings as Vincent and Connor, and she was getting it out of her system. "Yes, our job is to eat and listen. Hazel, I understand something happened to you this morning?"

I groaned in response. "Can we eat first? I need to fortify myself for this tale."

Jo and Marlee agreed, and we put in our orders the next time Valerian zipped past us. As Jo was telling us more detail about the intention she'd written for a quiet day at work, Barry came back inside the bar. It was unusual to see him there in the evening. He typically preferred the quieter hours during the daytime.

Instead of heading for his usual spot at one end of the bar, Barry lumbered toward us. "You ladies okay?" He was addressing all of us, but his eyes were on Jo. She nodded, looking grateful but also a bit shy.

"We're fine," I assured him. "Just mystified as to what all that was about."

Barry hitched up one shoulder. "When we got outside, Connor started babbling about how Vincent was doing things that vampire law prohibited, and he claimed calling Vincent out on it was for the good of everyone in town. He failed to give me details, though."

"Are you okay?" Jo asked, looking worriedly at Barry. The two of them had broken up months before I'd met either one, but it was clear there was still mutual affection between them.

"Connor didn't touch me. I followed him to his car and watched him drive off. Hopefully, he doesn't decide to come back."

Barry moved off to his stool, and Valerian wasted no time getting a glass of his favorite whiskey in front of him.

Our dinner showed up not long after, and once I had a turkey melt and fries in my belly, I waved Valerian over and quickly gave my coven an account of my incident at Stacy's Stationery and Sundries. When I was finished, Jo gave me a hug while Valerian and Marlee promised to help me do a spell for magical control soon.

"But I do those all the time," I protested.

"Exactly," Marlee said. "You do them. On your own. You need your coven's help, so we'll do a group spell."

"You'll have things under control in no time," Jo said.

"Thanks." I thought briefly of the angry faces I'd seen when I walked into the tavern that evening. That coven had radiated negative energy. They had felt spiteful, and my coven felt supportive. "I'm really glad I have all of you."

The next morning, I woke up to the noise of hurrying feet. It sounded like more than one person, and the dull tramp on the hallway carpet gave way to the pounding of shoes on the wooden floor of the kitchen.

Perkins had slept on the pillow next to my head, and he was wide awake, staring at my bedroom door. "What's going on?" I asked him. Of course, he couldn't answer, but even he seemed to sense something was amiss.

I threw back the covers and leaped out of bed as well as my middle-aged body could. Quickly, I grabbed my fuzzy bathrobe and pulled it on. I was still tying it around me as I walked into the kitchen. Perkins fluttered along in my wake.

Jo and Valerian were standing there, slightly out of breath. Other than that, everything looked fine.

"What's going on?" I asked, trying to spot anything amiss.

"That's what we'd like to know!" Valerian was in her pajamas, and her hair was wild. "I was sound asleep, and there was a huge crashing noise that woke me up."

I looked around. "You think it came from the kitchen?"

Jo nodded. "I heard it, too. I was in the bathroom, putting on my makeup, and the sound definitely came from this direction."

"I bet that's what woke me up, then, since my alarm hasn't gone off yet."

All three of us jumped when the doorbell rang. I laughed self-consciously. "You two keep looking for what made that sound. I'll get the door."

The kitchen was in a back corner of the house, so I had to traverse the hallway that ran along the rear of the house before turning into a wider, fancier hallway that led to the front door. That hallway had been the one seen by the public when the place was an operational funeral home, and it had a lush burgundy carpet and floral wallpaper.

I opened the door and was surprised to see Chief Constable Wyatt Hightower. His old sedan was parked out front, which meant he hadn't walked over from his house a few doors down. He was already dressed for work, and I could see the upper edge of his crisp gray uniform shirt peeking out from the top of his black jacket.

Suddenly feeling self-conscious about my own attire, I pulled my robe tighter around myself and crossed my arms. "Wyatt? What brings you here?"

"I was driving past, and some kind of shockwave hit my car. What sort of magic are you ladies working in there?"

"None. In fact, we're trying to figure out what happened, too."

Wyatt's ice-blue eyes shifted their focus to something behind me. "It was your poltergeist."

"Maybe." I shrugged. "You want some coffee to take with you to the station?" Being polite to Wyatt was a personal mission of mine, since he and I had been clashing with each other since we met.

Wyatt didn't answer. His face paled, and he ran a shaky hand through his silver hair before he stretched out his arm to point down the hallway. "Not maybe. I can see the ghost right behind you."

Chapter Four

I WHIRLED AROUND TO see what Wyatt was pointing at. Just a foot away, a shimmering, vaguely human shape was hovering in the hallway. I couldn't see any details, but I was certain this wasn't our regular ghost, Holman. We knew we had a second entity in the old funeral home because it had been causing all kinds of poltergeist activity. Things were being knocked off shelves and thrown by unseen hands.

Is this the thing that's been causing the problems? Am I in danger?

I sucked in my breath and recoiled in fear. That only brought me closer to Wyatt, and as my back made contact with his chest, he instinctively wrapped his arms around me.

Being so close to Wyatt was unnerving, and I felt an electric tingle run through my body. It wasn't all that different from the way the ATM had shocked me that morning, except Wyatt was a living, breathing human rather than a machine.

I let out a cry of distress as I realized what was about to happen. There was no time to move or to warn Wyatt. I felt a jolt of magic course through me, starting deep in my chest and radiating outward. My magic had suddenly built up in my fear and embarrassment, and it burst out of my body in a bright pink wave.

Wyatt let go of me, and I didn't feel his body behind mine anymore. In front of me, the shimmering entity seemed to grow brighter and more solid for a heartbeat before it disappeared.

The blast unbalanced me, and I reached out with both arms to catch myself in the doorway. Once I had my feet solidly underneath me again, I turned to check on Wyatt. He was standing a few feet away, on my front porch. The fact that he hadn't been knocked over was remarkable.

There was a look in Wyatt's eyes I had never seen before. It was something between surprise and fear.

Is he afraid of me?

Of course he is, a voice in my mind answered. *As he should be.*

I knew my cheeks were burning as I said haltingly, "I'm so sorry. It scared me to see it standing there, and my magic built up too fast for me to do anything about it, and I just, I just..." I stopped talking and bit my lower lip as I felt my throat constrict.

I am not going to cry in front of Wyatt. It had almost happened once before, and I was as determined now to keep my emotions in check as I had been then.

Wyatt's voice was low when he spoke. "It's not getting better, is it?"

He was talking about the spikes in my magic, I knew, and my ability to control them. I squeezed my eyes shut and shook my head. "I was improving, but it's been getting worse the last few months."

Wyatt and I were really good at getting on each other's nerves. We excelled at having silly disagreements, and I was convinced that he was the grumpiest person in all of Foxfire Haven. So, with that in mind, I steeled myself for the lecture he was about to give me, or maybe just a heavy sigh followed by a snide comment about having a lousy witch for a neighbor.

I was stunned, then, when Wyatt nodded once. "Just let me know how I can help. In the meantime, I have to get to the station."

Without letting me reply, he turned and headed down the steps. It wasn't until he was shutting the door of his car that I blurted out a stunned, "Thank you."

I was still standing in the doorway, staring in shocked silence toward the road, when I felt a gentle hand on my arm. "Haze?"

Marlee was standing just behind me, and I could see her worried expression when I turned to her. She must have heard the ruckus and slipped out of her bedroom to investigate.

"That was Wyatt," I said.

"You're not angry." Marlee narrowed her brown eyes at me thoughtfully. "You're not upset. It's more like... Hmm. You feel overwhelmed."

I let out a shaky laugh. "That's one way of putting it."

"Putting what?" It was Jo, who was coming down the hallway with Valerian in tow. "Val and I felt your magic. Who was that at the door, and what did they do to make that happen?"

"It was Wyatt," Marlee said. She said his name like it left a bad taste in her mouth.

"Wyatt isn't the reason I had a magical exhalation," I said quickly. "He was actually really nice to me. He and I saw the other ghost, and that sent my magic soaring."

That, and being pressed up against his chest with his arms around me, I added silently.

The other three women gasped. "You saw the poltergeist?" Valerian asked. "It had a beard, right?"

Uncle Grant had left a lot of photos lying around the funeral home, the garage, and even inside the hearse itself. In one shot of the casket sales room, there had been a transparent man with dark hair and a beard. We assumed that was the ghost causing the poltergeist activity. I certainly hoped that was the case, and that we didn't have a third ghost wandering the house.

I described the shimmering form Wyatt and I had seen, adding that it was humanoid but not distinct enough for me to recognize any features.

"Wild," Jo said when I'd finished.

"If that ghost rattled the whole house this morning and took corporeal form, it's getting stronger," Marlee said.

Barry, of all people, had told us to expect that. He had said that as we got stronger as a coven, we would raise the energy inside the house, and the poltergeist would be able to use that energy like a battery. We had done several spells to try to tamp down the excess energy in the atmosphere, but we weren't willing to do anything that would risk Holman's ghostly existence. He was a real pill sometimes, but we certainly didn't want to get rid of him.

We moved to the kitchen so we could settle around the breakfast table and discuss our theories over coffee.

We even tried calling on Holman to join the discussion, but he didn't show. Since he was a self-appointed fashion critic, we had gotten him to materialize a time or two by putting on ridiculous outfits. Unfortunately, Holman had learned that trick and wasn't falling for it anymore.

Eventually, Valerian returned to her bedroom, and Jo left for work. Marlee declared she needed a shower and that any ghosts haunting the house were absolutely not allowed in the bathroom with her. My first delivery of the day wasn't until eleven o'clock, so I got started on some laundry and fed Perkins.

By the time I had finished my last delivery of the day, it was after five o'clock. I hadn't had a chance to stop for lunch, having to settle for a hastily eaten bag of potato chips in between shuttling things around Foxfire Haven for my clients. My first thought was that I could make myself an early dinner at home, but I felt a twinge of fear at that idea. I knew Marlee was meeting with a couple whose wedding she was planning, and Jo was still at the newspaper office. Valerian was already working at the tavern.

That meant I would be home alone with the poltergeist. Even though I had known we had one for weeks already, it had never bothered me that much. But, after catching a glimpse of the entity that morning, I was hesitant to be the only one at home if it showed up again.

Of course, our familiars were at home, so I wouldn't be truly alone, but I couldn't picture any of the birds helping me face down a ghost who liked to chuck things across the room.

So, with that in mind, I headed for the tavern. I could eat there, and seeing Valerian would help give me the courage I needed to head home afterward.

The tavern was mostly empty when I walked inside, and even Barry's stool was vacant. Only two other people were sitting at the bar, and I chose a stool that was far from them, so I could have a bit of privacy. Valerian pointed at me as I was getting settled. "You need my Nerves of Steel potion," she stated.

"How did you know that, Val?"

"Because you're here instead of at home, relaxing. You're not excited about having alone time with the sparkly poltergeist."

"You're absolutely right."

We had been talking loudly enough that the person nearest me at the bar heard us. He turned in my direction, a bright smile on his face. If he was trying to be friendly, he was failing miserably. There was something about his intense green eyes and the way he raised his eyebrows at me that felt slightly sinister. "Isn't Val the best? Valerian Bellamy, Foxfire Haven's best bartender! The first time I came in here, she had the perfect potion for me. Where else in this town can you get magic elixirs and great company?"

Valerian had her back to the bar as she prepared my concoction, but I caught the slightest shake of her head.

No sooner had Valerian put the glass of orange liquid in front of me than the man called her name. "Hey, don't forget us over here! I wanted to tell you about my cabin out on Lake Lonesome."

I could clearly see the discomfort in Valerian's expression. She briefly made eye contact with me before slowly walking to the other side of the bar. She stood back from it, I noticed, with her arms across her chest. Usually, she would lean against the bar, like the ideal friendly bartender. "What about it, Harris?"

The man launched into a story about his cabin, dropping several hints that he would very much like Valerian to see it for herself. His tone and expression conjured up a horror-movie scenario in my mind. Talk about "stranger danger."

I slowly sipped the potion, which had a pleasant citrus tang to it, while keeping an eye on my friend. When Valerian finally got a moment to check on me, I mouthed, "You okay?"

Valerian gave a brief nod, and I said casually, "I was thinking about sticking around here for a bit, even after I eat something. You know, so I can continue avoiding the poltergeist."

"I think that's a good idea." I could tell by Valerian's tone that she understood I wasn't suggesting I stay at the tavern because I was afraid to go home, but because I didn't want to leave her alone there.

I put in an order for a sandwich, and long after I had eaten it, the man—Harris, Valerian had called him—was still trying to chat her up. The more he drank, the more suggestive his comments became, and the more Valerian retreated into herself, until she was barely acknowledging his presence. The guy really didn't know how to take a hint.

I had finished my potion and moved on to nursing a diet soda when someone came into the bar and chose a stool between Harris and me. I gave the man a brief glance, then quickly looked again. It was the vampire who had gotten into a fight there just the night before. If Vincent was there, then I sure hoped Connor the werewolf wouldn't show up, too.

Valerian was apparently thinking along the same lines. "Didn't we kick you out of here last night?" she asked.

"No one said I couldn't come back," Vincent countered. "Can I have a Type O, please?"

Without a word, Valerian retrieved a metal flask from a cooler underneath the bar. I didn't think I would ever get used to seeing vampires drink blood in public, but at least the flask hid the contents.

Vincent took a sip, then winked at Valerian. "It would be better directly from your neck, of course. I bet you taste divine."

CHAPTER FIVE

HARRIS WAS ON HIS feet and moving toward Vincent so quickly I wondered if he might be a vampire, too. But, no, he had been drinking cocktails made from Valerian's potions, so he was something else. A witch, probably.

When Vincent turned to face Harris head-on, his back was to me, but I noticed how casual his stance was. He didn't even bother to get off his barstool. "You got a problem with vampires?" he asked smoothly.

"I have a problem with anyone who threatens this woman." Harris was now so close to Vincent he couldn't have gotten off his stool if he had wanted to. He was effectively pinned against the bar.

Vincent laughed quietly. "I wasn't threatening, you idiot. I was flirting. I'm sure she knows the difference."

My eyes flicked to Valerian, who was watching the scene with her hands on her hips. She looked fed up, but I also saw the ghost of a smile on her face. She glanced at me, winked, then returned her attention to the two men. "Out! Both of you!"

That got the disagreement between Harris and Vincent to stop immediately. Instead, they rounded on Valerian and began to protest. Harris declared he was only looking out for her, while Vincent said it wasn't his fault that the other guy couldn't tell a pick-up line from a threat.

Valerian pointed at Vincent. "If that was a pick-up line, then you're going to have a hard time finding anyone to go out with you. We just kicked you out last night, and now you're back, causing trouble. I won't have it." Her arm swiveled until her finger was pointed at Harris's chest. "And you instigated things, so you're out of here, too."

"Oh, come on, I was doing something chivalrous for you," Harris said, his voice oily smooth. "Besides, I haven't even paid my tab."

"It will be waiting for you the next time you're here," Valerian promised. "Both of you go, now, or I will call Will out of the back to take care of things."

Vincent responded by leaning over the bar, then blowing a kiss at Valerian and baring his fangs. "Next time, then. I'd still like a taste."

Harris lunged toward Vincent at that, but when Valerian shouted Will's name, the two of them quickly headed for the door.

Once the door had closed behind them, three people in a booth along one of the walls began to clap. A woman at a table shouted, "Go, Val!"

Valerian did look pleased with herself, but she also seemed slightly shaken. "Twice in two days," she muttered as she moved toward me. "Thanks for sticking around to keep an eye on me."

"You're okay?" I asked.

Valerian was one tough witch, and it was rare for anything, or anyone, to get under her skin. However, she hesitated before answering, "I think so. That guy Harris used to come in here once in a while, and he's always been weirdly flirtatious with me, but after trying my Brighter Days Ahead potion one night, it was like he got obsessed."

"With the potion, or with you?"

"Both, I think. He's constantly dropping hints about wanting to spend time with me, and it's always mildly creepy stuff. Like, he told me his cousin is a taxidermist, and we should go tour his warehouse sometime."

"Ew."

"Exactly." Valerian lifted her hands and ran her fingers lightly over her head, beginning at the crown and working her way down to her neck. Then, she brushed each arm, from the shoulder to the fingertips. I knew she was silently reciting an incantation to rid herself of negative energy. "Can we do a spell later tonight? I'm thinking a boundary-setting spell."

I gave Valerian a little salute. "Your coven is here to help! I'm happy to stop by the magic store, if we need anything we don't already have on hand. It will save you a trip, and it will keep me from having to head home just yet."

"Let me think about that while you finish your soda." Valerian moved off to help a couple of customers who had just walked through the door.

A few minutes later, Valerian came up to me and said simply, "Yarrow. We're out of it, because we used the rest of what Marlee had in that success spell we did last week. Oh, and while you're at the store, can you please pick up a small piece of hematite for me? I'll carry it in my pocket as an extra bit of warding."

I agreed, then paid my bill and left. Into the Cauldron was just a few blocks down from the tavern, so I left the hearse parked where it was and walked. There was a light drizzle, with featherlight raindrops that shimmered in the streetlights, so I kept my hands stuffed in my pockets and my chin buried deep in my scarf.

Into the Cauldron was the only magic store in Foxfire Haven. On the one hand, it seemed surprising that a supernatural town only had one store for herbs, crystals, scrying bowls, cauldrons, and other items for working magic. At the same time, the town was so small I wasn't sure we could support a second shop. A high percentage of Foxfire Haven residents were witches, but our town's population was small.

The one downside of offering to stop by the magic store was that it was already dark out, which meant there was a good chance I'd run into Adeline Beaumont. Since she was a vampire, her staff ran the place during the day, and she worked the night shift. I had once suspected Adeline of having a hand in a local man's murder, and she had caught me snooping around outside her office window, which looked out into the alley that ran behind the buildings on that side of Main Street.

Adeline never figured out what, exactly, I had been doing out there in the alley, but she knew it hadn't been anything good. I would never admit I'd been trying to eavesdrop on her when an amplification spell I'd done to boost my hearing had backfired, amplifying my magic instead. That had been one of those magical exhalations that wasn't dangerous, but it had been incredibly embarrassing.

Before I pulled open the glass door that led inside the shop, I paused and did a quick shedding spell. There was no way I was going to risk an exhalation inside Into the Cauldron, because the place was absolutely crammed with products, and I couldn't afford to pay for anything I might break.

When I walked into the shop, I didn't see any sign of Adeline, and I hoped she was in her office rather than manning the cash register. Once I got past a rotating rack full of seed packets for various magical plants, I looked to my right. A man who looked like he was in his sixties was behind the counter, ringing up purchases for a young woman with blue hair.

I relaxed immediately and proceeded to track down the yarrow Valerian had requested, then went in search of the hematite. Soon, I had both items in hand, and I headed for the cash register.

Before I could put the items down on the counter, though, I heard an all-too-familiar voice coming from somewhere nearby. It was Vincent, and I only caught part of what he was saying. "...surely you have that stashed away somewhere. It's not illegal."

"No, it's not illegal, but it is unethical." Adeline's voice was raised slightly, and she had a weary tone, like it wasn't the first time she'd had this discussion with Vincent. "You know there are laws governing magical practices, and witches take that very seriously. If you're dabbling in witchcraft, you'd be wise to follow suit."

"I'm more than a century older than you, Adeline. Don't lecture me."

"Then don't ask me for items you know I don't carry."

"I can find someone else to sell it to me, but I'm trying to support my local small business." Vincent's voice had a tone like the one he'd used when he said he wanted to taste Valerian's blood. He spoke softly, but there was an underlying danger, like he was daring Adeline to retort.

A quiet voice behind me said, "Excuse me, are you checking out?"

Another customer had lined up behind me, so I hastily threw the yarrow and hematite on the counter and paid. As I was walking toward the door, I heard Adeline tell Vincent that he needed to leave, immediately.

How many places can the guy get kicked out of in one day?

By the time I pulled into the garage out behind the funeral home, I had decided I'd rather see the unidentified ghost again than Vincent. The vampire was that unnerving. At least, I knew, I wouldn't be home alone with the entity. Marlee's and Jo's cars had been parked out front, in the circular driveway.

The kitchen was full of laughter when I walked through the back door. Marlee was nearly doubled over in front of the sink while Jo was supporting herself on the countertop, her eyes squeezed shut in mirth. Gordon, Jo's pelican, was making loud cries while strutting along the kitchen floor. I could see a few limp strands of spaghetti draped over his beak.

"Jo, did your familiar just eat our dinner?" I asked as I took off my coat and hung it on a hook near the door.

Jo nodded. "Good thing we have more."

Marlee slowly stood up straight. In between giggles, she said, "I had just drained the pasta, and I turned away for one second to grab the bowls. Gordon swooped in and gobbled it all up in one go!"

"Gordon," I said, looking at the bird sternly. "You're going to teach the other familiars bad manners."

Gordon snapped his beak and gulped, swallowing the spaghetti while staring back at me. It was like he was saying, *And what are you going to do about it?* The situation was so ridiculous I began laughing, too.

By the time we had remade the spaghetti and gotten dinner on the table, we had fed the rest of our familiars so they wouldn't be tempted by our pasta. Valerian had gotten home by then, too, so she was able to join us.

We were just finishing up dinner when the doorbell rang.

Marlee grinned at me. "I bet it's your boyfriend again."

"Wyatt is not my boyfriend," I said. Marlee had been teasing me about that for months, though it had been a while since I'd heard her say it. "But I will go get the door, because Wyatt does seem to be our most frequent visitor."

After our odd encounter, both with each other and with the ghost causing the poltergeist activity, I wasn't sure how I felt about seeing Wyatt. He had been so kind with his offer of help, but I had also been mortified when I shed my magic all over him.

"Oh, let's just get it over with," I told myself.

I opened the door, fully prepared to see Wyatt standing there. Instead, it was a shorter man who looked like he was in his late fifties. He had wispy gray hair that was pushed back from his high forehead and intense, slightly wild eyes.

The man was familiar, but I couldn't quite place him. As soon as I heard his smooth voice, though, I realized I'd seen him just a couple hours before, at the tavern.

Harris gazed at me with expectation. "I'm here to see Valerian."

CHAPTER SIX

ALARM BELLS STARTED GOING off inside my head. I knew for certain Valerian hadn't invited Harris to stop by, and there was no way she had told him our address. Harris was giving off creepy stalker vibes, especially with the way he was leaning sideways to gaze down the hall with a look of hope.

Harris began to take a step forward, but I planted my feet and spread my arms. "Is Val expecting you?"

"I thought I would surprise her!" Harris was so close I could feel his breath on my cheeks. "It's more fun that way."

"I'm sorry, but this isn't a good time. I'm sure you'll see her at the tavern." I stepped back to close the front door, but Harris matched my movements, remaining just as close to me, so he was able to step over the threshold. He had made sure I couldn't slam the door on him.

"Who's at the door?" It was Marlee's voice I heard behind me. She must have picked up on my feelings, because I could hear her concern.

"A tavern patron," I called over my shoulder, not taking my eyes off Harris. "He's just leaving."

"No, I'm not," Harris said easily, as if we were having a friendly conversation. "I'm here to see Val."

Apparently, Jo and Valerian had followed Marlee into the front hallway, because I heard Valerian behind me, too. While Marlee had sounded concerned, Valerian was undoubtedly angry. "Harris, what are you doing here?"

"I wanted to come see you, and to talk about my behavior at the tavern. I was trying to stand up for you to that vampire, but you took it all the wrong way. I need you to understand that."

It was taking everything I had not to push Harris out the door. I glanced past him as I thought that, picturing him moving backward onto the front porch but not falling down. I didn't want to hurt him, after all. My eyes saw the wooden boards of the porch, followed by the stairs down to the ground, but there was nothing in view beyond that. A thick fog created a gray wall that glowed softly in the porch light, and it came right up to the foot of the stairs. The driveway and yard beyond were hidden in its depths.

There hadn't been any fog at all when I'd initially opened the door. I was certain of that. How had it appeared so suddenly?

I gave my head a sharp shake. I could wonder about that later. First, we had to get Harris out of the house.

Valerian walked up, standing just behind my shoulder so she could glare at Harris. When I glanced at her, I saw that her raven, Lonnie, was perched on her shoulder. "How do you know where I live?'

"It's a small town. Everyone knows you live at the old funeral home."

Okay, he had a valid point on that one. Still, Valerian was undaunted. "And why couldn't we have this conversation at the tavern?"

"I wanted to talk to you about it in private. Can we go sit down somewhere?"

"No. Please leave. I had to kick you out of the tavern because you were trying to start a fight with someone, and I do not appreciate you showing up here."

"Val, come on..."

I opened my mouth to reiterate Val's request, but before I could speak, I caught the faintest shimmer in the air in front of me. For a split second, I worried I was having a magical exhalation, but this shimmer had a white glow to it, not pink, like my magic.

The shimmering form shot away from me and slammed into Harris's chest, sending him reeling backward. He stumbled onto the porch, and then the front door slammed of its own accord.

We had gotten used to our front door opening by itself, and we had decided it must be the poltergeist responsible for it. There was no doubt in my mind that was who had just kicked Harris out of the house.

Valerian sucked in her breath while Lonnie let out a loud caw, but I gave a short laugh. "If the poltergeist would do things like that instead of throwing stuff across the room, I'd like it a lot more."

"You think the poltergeist did that?" Jo asked. "I thought I saw something shimmery in front of you, Haze. Was that the entity?"

I nodded. "It sure was. I guess we should check to make sure Harris didn't get hurt?"

Valerian opened the front door a crack, then shut it with a bang and locked it. “He’s fine, and he’s leaving. I guess he finally got the message. But he’s going to have a hard time driving home in this fog.”

“I think that’s my fault,” Marlee said. We all turned to her, and she smiled self-consciously. “When I felt Hazel’s fear, I knew whoever was at the door was someone we didn’t want here. I wished we were hidden, so someone bad couldn’t find us.”

“You conjured the fog,” Jo said. While Marlee’s strongest magical ability was her empathic nature, she was also quite skilled at weather magic. She had told us it came in handy in her job as an event planner, because she could keep rain away from an outdoor wedding venue, at least for a short time.

“I expect the fog ends right at our property line,” Marlee said. “It’s been years since I unintentionally caused a weather event.”

“And I thought my magical farts were dramatic,” I joked. Then, my tone turned serious as I said, “Val, are we going to have to get a restraining order on that guy?”

Valerian shrugged. “It’s bad enough seeing him at the tavern. The way he looks at me is just icky, and all of his comments about taking me to those creepy spots gives me chills. If he ever shows up here again, we’ll give him more than a spectral shove out the door.”

I lifted my head toward the ceiling. “Thanks, ghost. We don’t know who you are, but we appreciate your help with that guy.”

“And here I had thought we were in a battle with the poltergeist.” Marlee was looking around thoughtfully. “Whose side is it on?”

"We won't figure it out standing here," Jo said. "Let's have a cup of tea."

"And then we're doing my boundary spell," Valerian added.

As we filed down the hallway in the direction of the kitchen, Marlee said softly, "Now that I think of it, I commented on the wind a couple weeks ago while talking on the phone with a client. They were only a couple miles away, but they said the leaves outside were perfectly still."

Valerian put a hand on Marlee's arm. "Don't sweat it. The fog was a nice touch, and you were trying to keep us safe."

Before bed that night, we asked our familiars to take up watch, one on each side of the house. I moved Perkins's flannel nest from its spot by the radiator to the breakfast table. That wasn't quite high enough for Perkins to see out the side window there, so I added a stack of books, then perched the nest on top. It was perfect: my burrowing owl could see outside while also being snug in his nest.

Lonnie was posted on the front porch, and since Valerian's room was just inside the front door, she was in close proximity to her witch. Gordon settled into a spot on the back porch, after Jo had removed the last bits of spaghetti from his beak.

That left Marlee's toucan, Stella, to watch the opposite side of the house from where the kitchen and my bedroom were. Since she was a tropical bird and not built for cold Washington nights, Marlee set up Stella on the back of the couch in the living room, so she could gaze out the window there.

We went to sleep, trusting that if Harris had the nerve to come back, our familiars would sound the alarm.

Much to our relief, though, nothing did happen. We woke up the next morning and rounded up the birds, telling them they had done a great job and that they could take a well-earned snooze. Stella and Perkins curled up together in the flannel nest, Lonnie disappeared into Valerian's room, and we later found Gordon asleep on the bathroom rug. Apparently, he liked how fuzzy it was.

I only had two deliveries scheduled for that day, and both of them were in the morning. I went home afterward, no longer worried about being in the house alone with the poltergeist. I wasn't comfortable with the ghost just yet, but I was no longer worried I'd be hurt by it.

Valerian was working the early shift at the tavern, and all day, I kept my fingers crossed for her that Harris wouldn't show up and cause trouble. The first couple of times I'd texted her for an update, she'd said he wasn't there. When I texted a third time, she said she was still in the clear, and that Barry was perched on his usual stool. *I filled him in, and he's got my back*, Valerian had written.

After that, I stopped worrying.

In the afternoon, I was folding laundry, when my phone rang. I didn't recognize the number, so I answered, "This is Hazel with Dead Easy Delivery."

"Hazel, hi! It's Sophie at The Salt Circle Cafe. Do you have time for a delivery this afternoon? Someone just ordered a bunch of food for delivery. It says clearly on our website and on our menu that any orders for delivery have to be placed at least three days... Oh, never mind.

Anyway, none of us can get away to deliver the food, so I was hoping you might have time."

"You're in luck," I assured Sophie. "My afternoon is wide open. What time should I arrive?"

Sophie asked me to be there at four thirty, which was less than an hour away. I agreed, then returned to my laundry with a little more pep. It was an easy delivery job, and unexpected work was always something to be grateful for.

Especially now that I had those teacups to pay for.

I arrived at The Salt Circle five minutes early. There were no parking spots outside on the curb, so I swung around to a side street and found parking there. Luckily, I kept an old stainless steel gurney inside the hearse for transporting loads, so I got it out of the back and wheeled it to the cafe.

When I reached the front door, I paused, wondering if it was tacky to waltz into a cafe with a gurney that had once transported dead bodies through the funeral home. I turned and headed back toward the hearse, then cut down the alley behind the cafe. With all the trash and recycling bins, it would have been a squeeze to get the hearse down the alley, but the gurney and I fit just fine. I easily found the back door of the cafe and knocked.

A man I didn't know answered, and I introduced myself and my company. He immediately began to laugh. "I figured it was either Dead Easy, or my spicy chili killed someone. Come on in."

Sophie and the man helped me load all the takeout containers onto the gurney, then followed me to the hearse to watch me slide the gurney into the back of it. The wheeled legs popped up as I pushed the gurney against the back of the hearse, and Sophie gave an impressed, "Ooh!"

I nodded appreciatively. "It makes loading and unloading really easy."

Before they headed back inside, a woman walked up to them with a harried look. When she turned slightly to look at Sophie, I recognized her giant brown hair. It was the woman who'd been just inside the door of the tavern a couple nights ago, complaining that Adeline Beaumont was somehow responsible for a spell that had backfired.

And as soon as she began to speak, it was clear she still had a vendetta against the vampire. "Have you heard? The owner of Into the Cauldron is about to get what she deserves!"

CHAPTER SEVEN

SOPHIE GAVE THE WOMAN a sharp look. "Natalie! I know you're unhappy with Adeline, but what do you mean she's going to get what she deserves?"

Natalie rolled her shoulders back, and her sharp chin lifted proudly. "My coven and I did a spell against her. They wouldn't let me curse Adeline, but we agreed to do a karma spell on her. She deserves retribution for what she did to me, and she's about to get it."

"Get what?" asked the man, who was looking at Natalie with a slightly fearful expression.

Natalie tilted her head. "I'm not sure, exactly. If I knew the future, Gabe, I'd be a psychic, not a witch. But karma is coming for her, and I can't wait to see how it plays out."

Sophie frowned. "I've always tried to steer clear of magic that could cause harm to anyone else," she said carefully. It was like what I had overheard Adeline herself saying to Vincent about magical laws. *Do no harm* wasn't a guideline but a rule. Natalie was brave to be bragging about doing a spell that could cause bad things to happen to Adeline.

I got the impression Sophie didn't want to outright lecture Natalie, but she wanted to make a point, nonetheless. "I'm sure you'd feel awful if something bad really did happen to Adeline."

"No, I wouldn't. I'll raise a toast to her bad luck when it comes, and my entire coven will join me." Natalie was grinning now, clearly picturing a dark future for the vampire.

Again, I was struck by the difference between my coven and Natalie's. I had no desire to surround myself with such spiteful women.

"Natalie," I began. When she looked at me, she seemed surprised, as if she was just noticing my presence. "Do you anticipate bad things happening for Adeline because of the spell you and your coven worked, or is there more to it?"

"You haven't heard, then." Natalie looked around at the three of us, then leaned in, even though there was no one else on the sidewalk to overhear. "Rumor has it there's a hunter in the area."

Gabe recoiled, and he muttered a few sharp words under his breath. "No one told me about this," he said.

Natalie shrugged. "If you're not a shifter or a vamp, you have nothing to worry about. Hunters don't care about witches."

Like territorial disputes between werewolves and vampires, I had thought hunters were a thing of the past. They had flourished in Europe during the Middle Ages, often working for secret societies of non-magical people who had learned about the supernatural world. Hunters had been something we learned about in history class.

And Natalie was right about hunters not caring about witches. They had always gone after the more dramatic supernatural creatures, including the famous Troll of Culpepper Bridge. That story had become a regular campfire tale in our world.

"I'm a swan," Gabe said. He was glancing around nervously, though I was amused at the idea that the portly cook, whose white T-shirt was splattered with what looked like tomato soup, transformed into a beautiful, elegant swan during each full moon.

Natalie made a *tsk* sound. "You'd best be careful, then. The local were-guild should have some advice for you."

"Yeah. I'll go call them right now." Gabe wandered back toward the rear entrance of the cafe, already pulling his phone out of his pocket.

"Poor guy," Sophie said. "We'll all have to be on the lookout."

"You're hoping that this hunter tracks down Adeline," I said, returning my attention to Natalie. I didn't add the obvious conclusion of such a scenario. Did Natalie really want Adeline dead? Had her spell gone that badly that she considered death a just consequence? "She must have really hurt you somehow."

"I'm surprised you haven't heard the story." Surprised or not, Natalie was clearly eager to share the details with me. Her eyes lit up as she began, "I went to Into the Cauldron to buy supplies for a spell to make someone's rudeness be reflected back to them."

Sophie lifted a hand. "I have to get back to my tables, but I've already heard this story. Natalie, keep me posted on this hunter, please."

"Of course, of course." Natalie barely paid attention as Sophie walked away. "Adeline asked if I needed help, and I told her I wanted to get my hands on a bit of fresh-cut holly and the shed skin of a cobra. Well, Adeline, she gets all uppity about it and tells me that no one uses cobra skin these days. I said, yes, they do, including my coven. We don't do a negative reflection spell often, but when we do, we do it right! Adeline, she acts all offended, like she's never met a witch who dabbles in a bit of gray magic before. But she insisted she didn't stock cobra skin, and I'd have to find it elsewhere."

While Natalie paused to take a breath, I wondered how often Adeline had conversations with customers who wanted to do spells that fell into that area between positive magic and dark magic. Spells that were selfish, vengeful, or just downright petty were probably more common than I liked to believe.

"Anyway, we could use cat fur in a pinch, so I asked for some of that, instead. I know that pet groomer down the road sells trimmed fur to Adeline. Later, though, when we did the spell, the whole thing blew up. I mean literally: the contents of the cauldron exploded right out of it, absolutely covering my kitchen in stains that I'm still trying to clean up! And when one of my coven members took a closer look at the cat fur, she realized it was actually dog fur! When I confronted Adeline about it, she claimed it was a mistake because the two things look similar, but I know better. She purposely gave me the wrong ingredient to make my spell backfire. Because of her deception, the rudeness was reflected onto me, not the witch I was targeting!"

What a horrible woman. Natalie was really walking the line between gray magic and dark magic, and she was clearly a mean, spiteful witch. I wouldn't want to be on her bad side, because there was no telling what her coven might do to me.

Natalie had stopped talking, and she was clearly waiting for me to respond. While I wasn't friends with Adeline, I certainly wouldn't want anything bad to happen to her, and I definitely didn't like the idea of a hunter tracking her down. At the same time, I didn't want to say anything that might put me on Natalie's list of people who had offended her.

"I've had some big magical backfires, myself," I finally said, deciding that sympathy was the safest route. "I can't imagine how frustrating it was for you when the contents of the cauldron went all over your kitchen."

"White cabinets spattered with black ink! My tile floor covered in sap from the holly branch we used! Just awful!"

I nodded and made noises of agreement. Then, I said, "Natalie, it was nice to meet you. I've got to get this food delivered, but I'll keep an ear to the ground for news about this hunter."

"You do that. In the meantime, I'm going to the magic store. I know Adeline won't be there since the sun hasn't set yet, but I plan to be waiting when she shows up!" Natalie gave a laugh that was borderline cackle, and I wrinkled my nose at her back as she walked away, her head still held high and a bounce in her step. The woman didn't seem to feel at all guilty for the kind of magic she was working.

Just as Valerian had done at the tavern, I brushed myself off, running my hands from the top of my head down to my legs while visualizing any negative energy from Natalie sliding off my body. Most of the people I had met in Foxfire Haven were kind. Natalie was one of the rare exceptions.

Luckily, the food in the back of the hearse consisted of sandwiches, a tub of coleslaw, bags of potato chips, a tray of brownies, and several gallons of iced tea. I didn't have to worry that anything had gotten cold while I'd been talking to Natalie.

The address for the delivery was on a street I didn't know. When I looked it up on my phone's map, I realized why. Comet Drive was nearly to Brentwood. I headed south on Main Street, and soon, Foxfire Haven had given way to fir trees. I made three turns before arriving at Comet Drive, and with every turn, I felt like I was getting farther and farther from civilization, even though I was only a few miles from downtown.

As I pulled into a long drive, I got a distinct feeling of loneliness. The house I eventually pulled up to was a nicely maintained white clapboard Victorian, but it was set between two steep hills, and the late-afternoon sun had already dropped below the line of fir trees that dotted the Western hill. Fog was beginning to roll in, too, though not nearly as thick as what Marlee had conjured. Even though several cars were parked along one side of the drive that ran toward the back of the house, the world felt empty and quiet as I opened the door of the hearse and climbed out.

My loneliness disappeared as I was unloading the gurney. A delivery van pulled up behind me, and the driver hopped out. He was, inexplicably, wearing shorts despite the cold. "Shawna Sullivan?" he asked. "I've got seven packages for you!"

"No, I'm not Shawna. I'm making a delivery, too." I gestured toward the boxes stacked on the gurney.

"Cool delivery vehicle," he commented before heading to the back of his own, much-less-cool delivery vehicle.

I rolled the gurney to the foot of the stairs leading onto the wide front porch, then made my way to the front door. Before I could knock, it opened, and a woman I assumed was Shawna stood there. She wore thick-rimmed cat's eye glasses, and her hair was in long brown pigtails. Her slouchy tan sweater and long green skirt gave her a bohemian air.

"Yes! We are starving!" Shawna deftly moved past me and made a beeline for the gurney.

"I can help you take everything inside," I offered.

"Oh, sure, you can drop the food on the side table just inside the door." Shawna was already scooping up the sandwich boxes. "We've been so busy we didn't have a lunch break today, so we're having an early dinner."

"You work from home?" I guessed as I grabbed the brownie tray.

"Yeah, I make pre-packaged potions and spell bundles. You know, so you can buy everything you need for a spell at once. But orders have been picking up since people got word of a hunter in the area." Shawna led the way up the stairs and into the entryway. As we both put down our bundles, she continued, "That's why the delivery guy is here. I'm restocking items to use in magic that will hold off hunters. Protection spell bundles, ready-made potions to go unnoticed, that sort of thing."

Gabe at The Salt Circle might want a pre-packaged protection spell, I thought.

"I just heard the rumor before coming here," I commented.

"It's wild, right? A hunter, in Washington, in this day and age! Practically unheard of. I've got five people here helping me get spell bundles put together."

I carried in the last of the food while Shawna began to bring in all the packages she'd just received. The man delivering them probably had no idea the contents were for magic. I hadn't even known about Shawna's business, despite living in the same town as her. Every time I thought I'd relearned my way around Foxfire Haven, I was surprised by something new.

When I was finished unloading the food, I wished Shawna luck with her sales and headed back toward Foxfire Haven.

The talk of protection spells made me think of Valerian and her unwanted visit from Harris. We had done a boundary-setting spell for her, but more magic couldn't hurt. I could pick up a few items at Into the Cauldron for a protection spell.

It was already dark when I walked inside the store, and once again, I paused to listen for Adeline's voice. All I could hear, though, was quiet instrumental music playing on overhead speakers. I needed malachite for the spell I had in mind, so I made my way to the appropriate aisle.

When I got there, I saw that a box of rose quartz crystals had been knocked off one of the shelves. The crystals were strewn across the wooden floor, and one had rolled right into a pile of dirt.

No, not dirt. I crouched down to take a closer look. It was ash.

Nothing nearby was burning, but I knew this ash hadn't come from a fire.

I was looking at a dead vampire.

CHAPTER EIGHT

I INSTANTLY BEGAN TO argue with myself. Yes, I was looking at a pile of ashes, and that pile happened to be about the same size as the urn my mother had brought home after my grandfather's cremation and funeral. I reasoned that the magic store probably sold ashes for various spells, and a bag of them must have been ripped open by accident.

Then, somehow, the box of rose quartz had fallen off the shelf, sending tiny spears of the pale-pink rocks tumbling into the ashes.

Suddenly, I wondered if Into the Cauldron also had a poltergeist.

Whatever had happened, I told myself I was not looking at the remains of Adeline Beaumont. Even if the rumor that a hunter was in the area was true, it was highly unlikely they had come into the store and staked Adeline right there in the middle of the crystal aisle.

"Hello? Did someone come in?" It was a woman's voice, deep and resonant, and I recognized it as Adeline's at once. She was definitely not a pile of ash.

"Um, hi," I called. "I'm just picking up a few things."

"Sorry. I was in the back office." Adeline's voice was closer now. "My afternoon clerk had to take off early, but I was—" Adeline cut off as soon as she stepped into the aisle and realized who she was talking to.

I pointed down at the floor. "It was like this when I came in," I said hastily. Then, in a gesture of goodwill, I added, "Would you like some help cleaning up?"

Adeline didn't answer me. I'm not even sure she heard me. She was staring at the pile of ash, and she slowly raised her hands to her cheeks. Her olive-colored skin usually looked beautiful, almost glowing, but in that moment, it looked slightly gray.

"It is a vampire, then," I guessed.

Adeline nodded slowly, her long silver hair falling over her shoulders. "But how? Who?"

I shook my head. I didn't have the answers to those questions.

Adeline's fingers curled until she was making fists, her hands still pressed tight to her face. "A vampire was killed in my store. No one has killed a vampire in this town for more than a century. I don't understand."

Adeline's usually firm voice was shaking, and I refrained from mentioning the rumor about the hunter. There was no need to make her worry that her life was in danger, too. Instead, I asked, "Do you want me to call the constables?"

"Constables?" Adeline repeated it like she hadn't really understood me. A few seconds later, without taking her eyes off the pile of ash, she nodded slowly. "Please. Yes. Thank you."

I took several steps back, reminding myself not to touch anything. Even that fallen box of crystals was evidence now. I had Wyatt's number in my phone, so I called him directly. He answered on the third ring.

"Someone killed a vampire," I told him. It felt so strange to say it out loud. Like Adeline had said, this kind of thing just didn't happen in Foxfire Haven anymore. It didn't happen anywhere, for that matter. The magical world was a much safer place than it had once been.

Maybe we had taken that safety for granted.

Wyatt sounded as stunned as I felt. "Are you sure?"

"Adeline says it's definitely a vampire. We're at Into the Cauldron."

"I'll send some constables immediately," Wyatt promised. "And I'll get there as soon as I can."

I hung up the phone and looked at Adeline. She was standing on the opposite side of the crime scene, gazing around her shop with a shocked look on her face. Her pale-green eyes were wide.

"The constables will be here soon," I told her.

"I have a security camera," Adeline mumbled. "On the front door. We'll be able to see who came in."

"Good," I said. "Do you think this could have been an accident?"

Adeline's head snapped in my direction. "Do you know how hard it is to kill a vampire? A wooden stake has to be driven directly into their heart. This vampire didn't accidentally impale themselves on a stick of incense." Her face twisted, and for a moment, I thought she was going to cry. Instead, she began to yell. "And to find you, right here where it happened! What are the chances of that? You probably did this yourself, and you're only pretending that you ran into it. You, of all people! The sneaky, weird little witch who doesn't know how to control her magic!"

It felt like a stake was being driven into my own heart. Metaphorically, of course. I knew Adeline didn't like me, but to hear her accuse me of murder and call me sneaky and weird hurt a lot more than I wanted to admit.

Wait until she hears about the teacups at Stacy's.

That reminded me I needed to tread carefully. My magic had to be building up inside me, between discovering the remains of a vampire slaying and Adeline being so mean, and the last thing I wanted was for it to let loose and disturb the crime scene.

Wyatt would never let me live that down.

So, before that could happen, I told Adeline, "Okay, I understand you don't want me here. I'll wait outside."

She didn't protest, so I quickly and quietly made my way to the front door. I was stepping onto the sidewalk just as two sedans with the Foxfire Haven Constables logo on them came to a stop on the curb.

I recognized one of the men, who had been at the funeral home with Wyatt when I had found a body underneath the hearse. "Callan," I said, a bit breathlessly. "Adeline is inside. The body, er, the ashes are in the crystal aisle. Go right inside the door, and it's the second or third aisle over."

Callan instructed the three other constables to go on inside. As soon as they had disappeared through the door, he asked, "How are you involved, Ms. Underwood?"

"I was just stopping by to get some items for a spell." I shrugged. "I saw the pile of ash, but I had convinced myself it was just something that spilled out of a bag or a box. When Adeline saw it, though, she knew what it was immediately."

Callan nodded. He opened his mouth, hesitated, then said, "Chief Constable Hightower will be here shortly. Will you please stay until he can talk to you?"

"Sure."

Callan went inside the store while I stood on the sidewalk, wondering if that had been his way of not having to deal with me. Wyatt had probably complained to Callan before that I always landed smack in the middle of investigations, but this was the first time I had found a body—ashes, I corrected myself again—since Steve Zillmann's body had been hidden in my garage. With my reputation, I figured, Callan was happy to let Wyatt handle asking me about my discovery of the vampire.

Although I couldn't be certain, I had a strong suspicion I knew exactly who that vampire was. Vincent had been in the store just the day before, when he and Adeline had been in a disagreement about the kind of magic he wanted to work.

Vincent had also gotten himself kicked out of Sit A Spell Tavern twice in two days. There weren't a lot of vampires in Foxfire Haven, and I expected that when Adeline and the constables reviewed her security camera footage, they'd see Vincent walk into the store shortly after sundown tonight, but he would never be seen coming back out.

While I waited for Wyatt, I debated texting the members of my coven to tell them what was happening. But, at the same time, I didn't want to tell them anything until I had something more concrete to share. With nothing else to do, I paced back and forth along the sidewalk.

When I heard a man's voice, I thought at first that Wyatt had arrived. Instead, it was two of the constables coming out of the store to retrieve a box from the back of a squad car. As the man was carrying it inside, his partner spotted me staring at it. "Tools for collecting evidence," she told me.

I should have remembered that from when my garage had been the crime scene, but I was feeling frazzled. I continued my pacing, and by the time Wyatt did walk up to the front door of the magic store, I was rubbing the palms of my hands together to warm them up. The chill night air was beginning to creep into my bones.

"It's always you, isn't it?" Wyatt said wearily in greeting.

"I'm not usually the one stumbling on the victim."

"We don't know yet if this was murder or an accidental death."

"Adeline says it's pretty hard for a vampire to get turned into a pile of ash by accident," I pointed out.

Wyatt sighed. "Yeah. And a dead vampire means there's no body to give us clues as to what happened. It's going to be that much harder to figure out who was killed, and by whom."

"Hopefully, the security camera has the answers you need."

"Hmph." Wyatt crossed his arms and peered at the front display window with his eyes narrowed. "You mean the one that was unplugged a short time ago?"

"This was definitely a murder, then, and it wasn't a spur-of-the-moment decision on the killer's part."

Wyatt looked at me, and I thought I detected just a hint of pride in his voice as he said, "That's right, Hazel.

Someone went into the magic store with the intent to kill. Callan called me just before I got here and told me about the camera."

"The afternoon clerk had to leave early," I said, thinking back to Adeline's comment earlier. "Adeline was doing something in her office when I walked into the store, so no one was up front."

Wyatt had a notebook and pen in his hands so fast I almost asked if he was a magician. It was like they had just appeared. "And what time was this?" he asked as he quickly jotted down notes.

"A bit after six thirty, I guess."

"Not too long after sundown," Wyatt muttered to himself. After a moment, Wyatt stopped writing and peered at me again. "What else do you remember?"

"Just the pile of ash and the box of rose quartz crystals that had been knocked off the shelf nearby. Some of the crystals landed in the ashes."

"So, the box fell after the vampire was staked. Interesting. The vamp might have gone down swinging, or the killer was in a rush on their way out and knocked into the shelf."

"Also, I have a guess about who the victim is. There's this vampire named Vincent who got kicked out of Sit A Spell twice in the past two days. I heard him in here yesterday, and he was having a pretty intense discussion with Adeline."

"Are you accusing Ms. Beaumont of murder?"

I sucked in my breath. "What? No! No, I'm accusing Vincent of being a troublemaker everywhere he goes. In fact, the werewolf at the tavern on Tuesday night accused him of being up to some underhanded things, and then they started to fight before Barry broke it up."

A grin spread across Wyatt's face. It was the last thing I had expected to see while standing on the edge of a crime scene.

"What?" I asked.

"Your magic was at work before the murder even happened. You've been collecting clues for at least the past two days."

"That is," I said, "if Vincent is the victim."

As if on cue, the front door of the shop opened, and Callan walked out. He looked relieved to see that Wyatt was taking care of questioning me. "Chief Constable, we've identified the victim, if you'd like to come inside."

"His name was Vincent," Wyatt said with confidence.

Callan looked stunned. "How did you know?"

"Because Hazel just told me."

I felt a glow of pride warming me from the inside out. When Wyatt turned to me, though, his smile disappeared. "Hazel, no. Not here, not now."

I glanced down and saw a light-pink aura around my body. I squeezed my eyes shut and immediately began to recite a shedding spell, but it was too late. Wyatt's arms closed around me, and he pulled me tight against his chest as my magic slammed into him.

CHAPTER NINE

EVEN AS THE MAGIC left my body, I felt Wyatt pivot, spinning us both so his back was facing the magic store. That kept the glass of the show window safe from the shockwave, but it meant there was no barrier between the street and me. Somewhere nearby, a car alarm sounded.

When the alarm stopped its harsh clanging, the world around me felt oddly silent. I could feel Wyatt's chest rising and falling beneath my cheek, and his arms were still gripping me tightly.

Then, a sound came. A soft whimper, followed by another.

It was coming from my own mouth. *I will not cry in front of Wyatt,* I told myself. Except, it was too late. I could feel the tears springing from my eyes. Instead of pulling away from Wyatt, I lowered my head and pressed my forehead against his chest, trying to hide my tears and get myself under control before he noticed. I focused on taking deep, steady breaths.

Wyatt finally let me go, and I stepped back. I hastily wiped at my eyes before looking up, not at him but just over his shoulder. I wasn't ready for eye contact at the moment. "I'm so sorry," I said thickly. "Did I hurt you?"

Wyatt pressed a hand to his chest, his fingers splayed. "Your magic packs a punch, but I'm okay." He brushed at a bit of pink that was clinging to his silver badge.

"How did they identify Vincent when he was just a pile of ash?" I asked. I wanted to talk about anything that didn't have to do with my magical exhalation. Not only were they becoming more frequent and harder to control, but I had already realized that being around Wyatt seemed to spike my magic the same way strong emotions did. None of it was stuff I wanted to think about yet, let alone discuss.

"Callan?" Wyatt prompted.

Callan cleared his throat, looking at me uncomfortably. I scared him, I realized. "When a vampire is staked, their body turns to ash, but nothing else disintegrates. The killer must have collected the victim's clothing and other belongings before fleeing the scene. However, we found a credit card underneath the ash with the name Vincent Draxler."

"The killer probably grabbed Draxler's things, including his wallet, to keep us from identifying the ashes, not realizing there was a loose credit card," Wyatt speculated. "Draxler may have had it in his hand."

"He might have been heading to the cash register at the time of his murder, yes." Callan gave me another wary glance before asking Wyatt, "Then we're officially treating this as a murder?"

Wyatt nodded. "Yeah. I'll come inside and take a look." He turned to me and put a hand on my arm. "Are you okay to drive yourself home?"

I nodded. "All the excess magic has left me, so I'm fine. Thanks for keeping me from breaking the shop's window."

"Sure. Call me when you magically stumble onto more clues."

Wyatt really believed I had a skill for not just running into clues but for recognizing them as such. He thought it was part of my magic, an intuitive but magical ability to pull many threads into one cohesive story. I wasn't sure he was right, since the only magic I had ever shown any real aptitude for was in intuitive planning and organizing. I always seemed well prepared for even unexpected scenarios. And, to Wyatt, that meant I was good at organizing clues.

I drove home slowly, so lost in thought about everything that had happened in the past hour that I almost drove right past my own street. When I walked inside the back door, I saw Marlee standing in the middle of the kitchen, looking right at me. "Tell me everything, right now," she commanded.

"I'm giving off some pretty strong emotions, I guess," I answered.

"That, and Jo called to say there'd been a murder at Into the Cauldron, so she'd be staying late at the newspaper in case any news breaks about it. She heard that someone driving past saw you on the sidewalk in front of the store."

I hung up my coat, then sank down into a chair at the breakfast table. Perkins hopped over to me from his nest, fluttering up onto my shoulder. He tilted his head and rubbed it against my cheek, which was one of the ways he comforted me.

Marlee sat down opposite me, a sympathetic look on her face, and I dove into my story about finding Vincent's ashes in the crystal aisle, followed by my incredibly embarrassing exhalation. Marlee listened to all of it without saying a word, but halfway through my story, she reached across the table and took my hand.

When I was finished, Marlee gave my hand a squeeze. "What upsets you most?" she asked gently. "That you found a murder victim, that Adeline was mean to you, or that you shed your magic in a big way?"

That I shed in front of Wyatt, and that he had to grab me to keep me from doing harm.

For the second time that day, I felt tears welling up in my eyes. Marlee got up and moved so she was standing behind my chair, and she bent down and gave me a big hug from behind. "You're embarrassed, I know. We're going to work on this, as a coven."

"I'll start looking for stronger control spells tonight," I promised.

There was a loud bang behind me, and Marlee and I both turned to see what had caused it. The window next to the back door was open. We always kept it partially open, so our familiars could come and go, but the lower pane had been shoved all the way upward.

"Maybe the poltergeist is trying to say it approves of your plan?" Marlee squeaked.

"Whose side is this ghost on? It kicked Valerian's creepy stalker out of the house, but it keeps trying to scare us to death."

"Maybe, in addition to working a control spell, we also need to have a séance." Marlee didn't sound like she was keen on that idea, at all.

"Let's put that on the back-burner for the moment," I suggested. "Tonight, I just want to eat dinner, take a hot shower, and sleep."

The next morning, all three of my roommates were at the breakfast table when I shuffled into the kitchen. "Did Marlee fill you in?" I asked Jo and Valerian, then stifled a yawn. I'd slept fitfully, and my dreams had included Adeline bursting into flames while yelling that I was weird, Wyatt telling me to stop crying, and a monkey stealing my purse.

At least I had an explanation for the first two dreams.

"We know about your adventure at the magic store," Valerian said. "I'm sure you hated having one of your magical farts in front of your worst enemy."

That, at least, got a small laugh out of me. "Wyatt is not my worst enemy. We just don't get along well." Except, the past few times we'd seen each other, he'd been nicer than usual. Or was I just getting used to his grumpiness?

"I'm working the early shift today," Valerian told me, "but whenever I have a few quiet moments, I'm going to be looking through my grimoire. I'm going to modify one of my old spells to help you rein in your magic."

"I can write an intention for you," Jo said. When I opened my mouth to suggest that might not be a good idea, she raised her hands in defense. "I had a total manifesting win yesterday! My intentions sometimes work out great."

"What did you manifest?" Marlee asked.

Jo smiled proudly. "I wrote that I was going to eat a healthy but tasty lunch yesterday. I know that sounds silly, but I've been trying to eat better, and I'm not ashamed to use magic to help me do it. Not only did I have a delicious vegetable stew, but it was free! The owner of The Salt Circle had heard about most of the staff being out sick earlier this week, and since she figured some of them might still be recovering a bit, she sent over soup for all of us. Wasn't that sweet? Not only did I manifest a healthy, tasty lunch for myself, but I manifested it for the entire staff!"

"That's really neat, Jo!" I enthused. "It must be fulfilling to see your magic produce results like that."

"It is! I'm going to write another one today. Something similar in that it's not about anything super important, but still something that's exciting when it happens."

"Can you manifest Harris right out of town?" Valerian grimaced. "He showed up last night, an hour before closing, and talked my ear off the entire time. I almost called one of you to escort me home. I was *that* creeped out by him."

"You should have called us," I admonished. "I hate to think you left work last night feeling like you might be in danger."

Valerian waved a hand. "Oh, it all worked out. Wyatt stopped in for a late dinner after they wrapped things up at the crime scene, and he walked me to my car." She looked pointedly at me. "He really is a gentleman."

"Hmm" was all I answered.

I was saved from having to say anything more by the sound of Valerian's cell phone ringing. She dug it out of the pocket of her green cardigan and stared at the screen. "I don't recognize the number, but it's local."

"Let it go to voicemail," all three of us said in unison. Lonnie, the raven, followed that with a loud caw of approval.

"Your friends know not to call you so early in the morning," Jo pointed out. "Ordinarily, you'd still be asleep."

"Why are you up so early, anyway?" Marlee asked.

"I woke up with an idea for a potion themed around the spring equinox. It was so good I had to get out of bed and write it down, and by then, I was wide awake."

Jo stood and waved her empty coffee cup. "I'm going to get some more wake-up potion. Anybody need a refill?"

After Jo had topped up our coffee, Valerian's phone beeped to alert her to a new voicemail. She held the phone to her ear, and her expression darkened steadily as she listened. Her eyes flashed angrily, and she pressed her lips together. After a few moments, she threw her phone onto the table with a grunt.

"Val?" Jo prompted.

"Harris somehow got my phone number. He says he's worried about this alleged hunter in the area, and he wants to take me to his cabin to keep me safe."

I leaned toward her. "Val, you said you were going to modify a spell to help me control my magic, but I think you need to focus on your own situation first. We need to do a group spell to help Harris get over his obsession with you."

Valerian's eyebrows lifted. "I can think of one easy way to get rid of him, and that's if he's in jail."

"I don't think the constables will arrest someone for calling too early in the morning," Jo quipped.

"But they will arrest someone for murder," Valerian countered. "Remember, the day before Vincent was staked, Harris attacked him at the tavern."

Chapter Ten

"You think Harris killed Vincent?" I asked in disbelief. "Over his obsession with you?"

Valerian started to answer, then stopped herself. "No. I don't really believe that. It's just wishful thinking that I could easily get rid of him. He hasn't done anything to warrant a restraining order, and the idea that he might be locked up in jail and out of my hair is rather appealing."

"It would make the case an easy one for the constables, too," I said. "But I agree with you that Harris is likely innocent of staking anyone. Don't forget, Vincent was also kicked out of the tavern for fighting with Connor."

"He really had a beef with that werewolf," Valerian agreed. "He seemed to leave a trail of trouble wherever he went."

"Which means Harris, Connor, and Adeline are all suspects," Jo said. "That's three people just based on our own experiences. I imagine the official suspect list is much longer."

"Haze, I think you should call your boyfriend to tell him about Harris going after Vincent at the tavern." Marlee was trying to keep a straight face but failing utterly.

"I will gladly tell Wyatt," I said, emphasizing his name. "I'll call him later."

"Call him now," Valerian said, "and put him on speaker. I can give more details about Harris's behavior than you."

"I haven't even had a cup of coffee yet," I grumbled, but I pulled my phone out obligingly. Wyatt answered almost immediately, and before I put him on speaker, I asked if he had a few minutes to chat about the case.

"I'm about to leave for the station," he answered. "Should I just stop by?"

"We'll have a cup of coffee ready for you," I promised.

Less than ten minutes later, Jo was leading Wyatt into the kitchen while I finished making his coffee exactly the way he liked it, with one spoonful of sugar. "Good morning, ladies," he said. "I understand you all want to speak to me?"

"Just Hazel and me," Valerian clarified. "We're the two who have some information for you."

"I've got to get to the newspaper, so you can have my seat," Jo said, gesturing toward a chair at the table that was currently occupied by Gordon. She scooped him up in her arms and blew a stray feather off the cushion. "There you go."

Jo carried her pelican out of the kitchen, calling goodbye over her shoulder, while Wyatt sat down gingerly. He relaxed a bit when I set his coffee down in front of him with the assurance that I'd made it properly.

"Who would like to start?" he asked.

"There's this guy named Harris," Valerian began.

Wyatt's forehead creased. "Harris Kneale? He's trouble."

"Tell me about it. He used to come into the tavern once in a while, but he got really obsessed with my new Brighter Days Ahead potion, and he began coming in daily." Valerian paused and impatiently tossed her long braid over her shoulder. "At least, I thought it was the potion he was obsessed with."

"He wants to take you to his cabin for a quiet getaway." Wyatt said it with complete confidence.

Valerian sniffed. "I see I'm not the first to be invited."

Wyatt laced his fingers together around his coffee cup and stared into the dark liquid for a few moments. I got the impression he was carefully choosing his words. "Harris has never done anything illegal," he began, "but he does make a lot of people uncomfortable."

"And that's where I'm at with him." Briefly, Valerian described Harris's behavior at the tavern, and Wyatt nodded as if it all sounded familiar. When she reached the part about him showing up at the door of the funeral home, though, he stiffened. Valerian reached across the table and rested her fingers against Wyatt's jacket sleeve. "Don't worry. We got rid of him."

"We didn't," I corrected. "The poltergeist did. It shoved Harris onto the porch and slammed the door in his face."

That news didn't seem to reassure Wyatt in the slightest. He looked around the kitchen and grumbled, "I knew you were having some paranormal activity, but I didn't realize the ghost was that strong."

"Neither did I." The voice was that of our resident snarky ghost, Holman. The former funeral director had materialized in the kitchen doorway, and there was a frown under his pencil mustache. "It sounds like this other ghost is channeling enormous energy."

"Poltergeist activity is increasing, yes," I said.

Holman ignored me, instead fixing his translucent eyes on Wyatt. "Chief Constable, we meet again." He ran a hand down his light-gray suit, which was cut in the wide-shouldered and nipped-waist style of the nineteen thirties. "Can't you do better than that jacket?"

"No, I can't," Wyatt answered, his voice oozing sarcasm. "It's part of my uniform."

"Ladies, please help this man." Holman's head swiveled between Valerian, Marlee, and me. "Take him shopping. Find him a good tailor. Something!"

"Sure, Holman, we'll get right on that for you," Marlee said.

"Anyway, Hazel, I came here to tell you that it's only March, so change your shoes." Holman's lips pursed as he gestured toward my feet.

I was wearing a pair of white ballet flats, since I was just doing things around the house that morning. "Oh, don't worry. I'll put on much warmer shoes before I head out later."

"I don't care about how warm your toes are. It's before Memorial Day, which means all your white shoes should still be packed away."

"Holman," I said, mustering all the patience I could. "People don't really worry about that 'wear white only between Memorial Day and Labor Day' rule anymore."

"Maybe they should!" As Holman spoke, he slapped his palm on the table. But, since he was a ghost, his hand traveled right through the wood.

Except, I thought I detected just the hint of a vibration as his hand hit the table.

Before I could say anything about it, Holman disappeared.

"Sorry about him," I told Wyatt. "You know he only shows up to complain about how we dress."

"Did Holman have any choice words for Harris when he showed up here?" Wyatt asked.

"I wish," Valerian said. "Anyway, Harris left after the poltergeist pushed him out the door. Hopefully, he learned his lesson."

"I appreciate you letting me know about this," Wyatt said, "but I'm not sure how it ties into the case. Hazel said on the phone that's what you wanted to discuss."

Valerian raised her eyebrows and gave Wyatt a significant look. "Vincent started flirting with me at the tavern, and Harris started a fight with him."

Wyatt put his coffee cup down so quickly that a bit of liquid sloshed over the rim. He pulled out his notebook and pen. "Tell me every detail you remember, Valerian."

It took thirty minutes and two cups of coffee before Wyatt felt like he'd gathered every scrap of information he could.

Finally, Wyatt slid his pen and notebook into his jacket pocket and rose. "Thank you for this information, ladies. Valerian, you know I live just down the street. If Harris ever shows up here again, you call me immediately."

"Will do," she promised.

I saw Wyatt to the front door, but the only thing he said to me before he left was, "And you call me when you learn more details about the case."

He really thinks I have a knack for solving murders.

Marlee had quietly listened as Valerian and I spoke to Wyatt, and when I returned to the kitchen, she was leaning forward with her head down on the table. I rushed forward immediately, worried something was wrong, but Valerian held up a hand to stop me. *Overwhelm,* she mouthed.

Valerian looked worried, and I was pretty sure I did, too. We knew being in a place with a lot of people feeling strong emotions could overload Marlee. She would soak up all those feelings, leaving her overwhelmed emotionally and often weakened physically. But home was supposed to be a refuge for Marlee. Valerian had been a bit wound up about Harris, sure, but I felt like Wyatt and I had both maintained a sense of calm. What, then, had happened?

Valerian began rubbing Marlee's back. "Was it all three of us who sent you over the edge?"

Marlee lifted her head just a fraction. "I don't know. One of the feelings I got was loneliness, and I don't think that came from any of you."

"Maybe Holman is lonely," I guessed.

"It could have come from him," Marlee agreed. "Either way, I'm going out into the backyard to get rid of all these emotions that don't belong to me."

Both Valerian and I offered to accompany Marlee, but she said solitude would be best. She had an appointment that morning at Back to Realitea, the tea shop where one of her clients would be hosting a wedding shower, and she said being alone until then would be her best bet.

"What a weird morning," I commented after Marlee had walked out the door.

I felt bad for Marlee, but I understood that the best thing I could do for her was to simply steer clear, so I went about my morning tasks. She did pop her head into the office, where I was sitting behind a hulking antique desk, to let me know when she was leaving for the tea shop. She looked much better than she had at the breakfast table.

The rest of the morning was quiet. Valerian and I did a bit of cleaning, then I had a quick delivery for a client.

As I was driving home that afternoon, I was delighted to see the sun peeking out between the clouds. Spring was coming, even if the temperatures were still cool, and that meant we'd be getting more and more sunshine.

Except, as I got closer to my neighborhood, dark clouds suddenly formed in front of the sun, blocking out its light. I heard the rumble of thunder, followed by heavy raindrops that pounded against the windshield of the hearse. I had to slow to a crawl because it was so hard to see the street ahead of me.

I parked the hearse in the garage, then made a mad dash for the back door. Even still, my hair and face were wet by the time I got inside the house.

I knew what had happened as soon as I spotted Marlee, sitting with her head on the kitchen table again. "Marlee, honey, you're making it storm outside. The whole neighborhood is getting rain."

Marlee looked up. "Oh, no. I'm so sorry. It's just that Garth canceled on our date tonight. He said it's a family emergency, and I totally get that, but I'd been so looking forward to going out with him again, and it made me really sad, and—"

There was a flash of lightning outside, followed quickly by thunder.

I grabbed Marlee's hands. "Let's get rid of this storm, and then we can talk about Garth." Marlee had been on several dates with the gargoyle, and she was really enjoying getting to know him.

Before I began to recite a control spell, I squeezed Marlee's hands. "You know how the poltergeist is getting stronger as we raise the energy here?"

When Marlee nodded, I continued. "Holman made the table shake when he slapped it this morning, and he's told us time and again he can't manipulate physical objects. My magic is spiraling out of control. Jo's manifesting is getting really good but backfiring wildly, and Valerian's potions are so popular she's got that creep Harris breathing down her neck. It's not just us raising the energy for the ghosts. Something here is raising our energy, too. Our magic is growing, and none of us can control it."

CHAPTER ELEVEN

"FOG," MARLEE SAID.

I briefly considered that I'd misheard Marlee. Maybe she had uttered a bad word, instead. But, when I looked at her quizzically, she clarified, "I made it foggy to hide Val from Harris. And not long ago, I made it windy."

"Exactly. Up until now, you'd been consciously affecting the weather, like that time you gave us a dry patch out back so we could work a spell. Recently, your magic has grown so strong that you're doing it subconsciously."

"And if there is some kind of energy around here that's boosting our magic, it explains why yours keeps spiking."

I nodded grimly. "I have a hard enough time controlling it at its normal level."

"If you're right about there being an energy source," Marlee began, but at that moment, there was another crack of thunder. "Control spell, first. Then, we can discuss this theory."

Marlee's hands and mine were still linked, so I took a deep breath and began to say the incantation I used when I needed to slough off some of my magic. Valerian was the one who excelled at helping Marlee get rid of emotions that weren't hers, but since she was at work, I would have to do.

When I began to repeat the incantation the third time, Marlee joined in. By the end of the fourth recitation, the sound of rain against the windowpanes had softened to a quiet patter. Some dim sunlight streamed through the kitchen windows after six rounds, and I dropped Marlee's hands. "The sun is out again," I announced.

"Thanks, Hazel. I feel better. In fact, I feel so good that I think we need to have a coven meeting at the tavern, right now. I'll tell Jo she needs to head there, at least for a few minutes, and Val's customers will just have to wait while we fill her in."

"I'll drive," I offered.

The downside of taking the hearse anywhere was that it needed a lot of space for parking. There weren't any curb spots long enough for the hearse near the tavern, and we wound up more than a block away. During the drive, and my search for a parking spot, I had given Marlee some details about my energy theory, but it admittedly wasn't much.

Jo was just walking up to the door of the tavern as Marlee and I approached. She looked harried. "I am not having a good afternoon," she said.

"You're very frustrated," Marlee agreed. "Please, don't let me start a hailstorm on your behalf."

Jo's hand shot to the top of her head, and she ducked slightly. "Hail?"

"It's hypothetical hail," I promised. "Come on. We'll explain inside."

Thankfully, there were three stools next to each other at the bar. As we clambered onto them, Valerian stopped stirring a potion to stare at us. "Something happened."

"Something is happening," Marlee said. "Hazel figured it out."

"No, I have a guess, and we're as far from knowing what's going on as we could be." I turned to Jo. "First, though, why are you having a bad afternoon?"

Jo groaned. "Remember I said I was going to write small, unimportant intentions? This morning, I wrote that I would get to eat a great dinner tonight without having to do any of the cooking. Two hours ago, my editor came into my office to tell me I needed to write a piece of breaking news. The barbecue restaurant had a small kitchen fire, so I had to go there to get a couple of photos and do a quick interview with Garrett, the gargoyle who manages the place. He sent me home with free food."

Marlee laughed, but it was a soft, relieved sound. "That must be why Garth had to cancel our date tonight. He only told me it was a family emergency. I worried he was just making up an excuse because he didn't want to see me again."

"No wonder you made it storm, if you thought that," I said.

"First hail, and now a storm?" Jo asked. "And I'm sorry, Marlee. The fire is my fault, because my intention backfired, and I didn't even think about the fact that Garth works there, too."

"It's not your fault," Valerian insisted.

"Unfortunately, Jo's magic might have lent its energy to the fire," I said gently. "But I think I know why. Jo, your manifesting is taking off. Marlee subconsciously conjured fog when Harris showed up, and today, she made it rain when Garth canceled their date. Plus, she's been absorbing more emotions than usual."

"My potions have been wildly successful lately," Valerian said as her eyes lit up. "And your magical farts have been more like magical sonic booms."

"Our magic is growing stronger." I glanced around to make sure no one was listening to our conversation. The last thing I wanted was for what I was about to say to be repeated. "Barry said the energy we raised as a coven was fueling the poltergeist activity. But I don't think that's the full story. There's some kind of energy raising our magic, too, and I think it's somewhere inside the funeral home."

Jo, Marlee, and Valerian gazed at me silently. Jo looked thoughtful, while Valerian had a skeptical look on her face. Marlee, though, was staring at me intently. She was sitting next to me, and she laid both of her hands against my arm. I knew physical contact was a way for Marlee to get a better read on someone's emotions, so I remained still and silent.

After a moment, Marlee dropped her hands. "That makes sense."

"What does?" Valerian asked.

Marlee pointed at me. "Hazel is feeling curious and sad, which is a weird combination. She's curious about this mysterious energy source, but why would it make her sad? Because her uncle Grant lost his mind over it."

Jo gasped. "The rumor was that Grant was searching for some kind of treasure hidden on the property. But, like most gossip, that was a twisted version of the truth.

He was searching for some kind of energy vortex on the land the funeral home is built on."

"That's my theory," I said. "But keep in mind it's only a theory. I could be entirely wrong."

"But it gives us a good starting point," Valerian said. Her expression had changed to one of excitement. "I have divining rods somewhere. I haven't used them in years, but they can find energy just as efficiently as they can find water."

"And I have more modern-day equipment," Jo added. "Like a device that can detect electromagnetic frequencies."

I laughed. "Did you used to have a side gig as an electrician?"

Jo sat up proudly. "Oh, have I never told you three? I do some ghost hunting now and then. Ghosts are essentially just energy, so an EMF detector picks up their presence."

"Speaking of ghosts," I said, "I told Marlee that when Holman slapped the table this morning, I thought I felt it vibrate."

"I felt it, too, but I told myself it was just my imagination." Valerian picked up an empty pint glass and rotated it slowly in her fingers as she thought. "Holman has never been able to do that before, so his power is growing, too."

"Oh, no," Marlee said. "That's terrible! He'll start picking our outfits for us!"

All four of us laughed at that, and I felt some of the rising tension inside me loosen.

"What about our familiars?" Jo wondered. "Is Gordon going to start flying at light speed or talking?"

"I would love it if Stella could talk to me." Marlee began to list the various topics Stella might introduce in conversation, but she stopped when Valerian leaned toward us and hissed, "Heads up!"

At first, I thought she was warning me about my magic, and I looked down for any telltale signs of an impending explosion. Then, I heard Jo whisper, "We'll stay with you, Val."

It was Harris. He climbed onto a stool at the far end of the bar and waved at Valerian, as if nothing had happened between them whatsoever. "Val, honey, I need one of your pick-me-up potions. I just got raked over the coals at the constable station. Can you believe Hightower thought I killed that vamp? Ha!"

Valerian's face was neutral as she moved to make Harris's drink. "Oh?"

"Yeah, he heard about me coming to your defense, and he thought maybe I'd chased the vamp down and staked him over it. But why would I do something that stupid? If I wound up in jail, I wouldn't get to come here and drink your delectable concoctions."

"Wouldn't that be a shame," Valerian intoned. She passed the potion to Harris, then quickly returned to us. "Jo, I know you need to get back to work. Marlee and Haze, do you two care to be my security detail?"

"We're happy to hang out here for a while," Marlee said. "But we'll each need your Cold Hands, Warm Heart potion. Poor Hazel got soaked in my rainstorm."

"Coming right up."

Before long, Marlee and I were contentedly sipping on potions that made a warm tingle spread through our bodies. "No wonder Harris is obsessed with her," Marlee mused. "These are so good."

"Speaking of obsessed," I said, "you know all those photos we keep finding around the house? Uncle Grant seemed to be documenting every aspect of his life, but I wonder if he was trying to locate the energy."

"Or show some kind of change over time. You already put the photos in chronological order, thinking you might notice a pattern." Marlee pressed first one palm against the bar, then the other. "But, maybe, you were supposed to be looking for how things were changing."

"That's a good point. We all looked at Grant's photos without knowing what we were looking for, or even if there was something to look for. After all, he could have simply been a photography enthusiast."

"Like you said, though, the man was obsessed with finding something he believed was there on the property. This energy-well theory makes a lot of sense."

"I guess I know what I'm doing tonight, then. I'll pull those photos out of the shoebox I have them stashed inside."

Even as I said that, my phone rang. I pulled it out of my purse and looked at the number, but it wasn't one that was familiar to me. "This is Hazel with Dead Easy Delivery," I answered.

I heard a heavy sigh on the other end. "It's Adeline Beaumont."

Maybe she needs me to make a delivery for her store, I told myself. But that didn't seem likely when the woman disliked me so much. I couldn't keep the curiosity out of my tone as I said, "Hello, Adeline. How can I help you?"

"You can help me by proving that I didn't kill Vincent Draxler."

Chapter Twelve

How in the world am I supposed to prove Adeline's innocence?

It was a valid question. I barely knew Adeline, I had once suspected her of murder, and she very much disliked me. What made the woman think I could help clear her name?

Instead of pointing out any of those things, I decided to roll with Adeline's request like it was perfectly normal. "Tell me what you have in mind. Do you want to meet to discuss the case?"

Adeline sighed again, as if seeing me would be even more of a chore than talking to me on the phone. "I think that's a good start. Can you meet me at my store at six o'clock tonight?"

It was only then I realized it was barely five, and the sun had yet to disappear below the horizon. Adeline should have been dead asleep in a coffin, or an underground bedroom, or wherever she went to avoid the sunlight. I supposed even vampires got insomnia.

I agreed to the meeting time, and Adeline hung up after a curt "thanks." I turned to Marlee and Valerian with wide eyes and relayed her request for help.

"We figured she was a suspect, but I'm curious how she thinks you can help," Valerian said when I was finished.

"I'm as curious as you are. This is going to be an awkward meeting."

"Adeline's decent," Marlee said. "I'm in her shop all the time, and we get along just fine."

"She didn't catch you spying on her," I pointed out.

"True. But give her time. She'll come around."

"Think of it this way," Valerian said. "If you keep Adeline from going to jail for murder, she might just be your new best friend."

I grinned. "I already have three best friends, and I don't need any more. However, I do hope Adeline comes out the other side of this thinking better of me."

When I left the tavern nearly an hour later, Harris was still there and three drinks in. He'd been asking Valerian to turn each of the potions he was ordering into a cocktail, so I certainly hoped he was walking home that night. Marlee was still on guard for our friend, and Jo had texted to say she'd head over after work to keep Marlee company.

At least I was leaving Valerian in good hands.

The walk to Into the Cauldron was a fairly short one, but it seemed to last forever. My pace began to slow as I got closer to the shop, and my feet felt like they had weights dragging them down. I was nervous. I stepped into an alley just before reaching the store to shed any built-up magic inside me. It was a good thing, too, because there was plenty of it. I left behind a pink puddle that would slowly sink into the earth.

Adeline was behind the cash register when I walked into the store, and she was chatting with a customer who kept repeating, “Oh, bless your heart.” When the woman turned and left, Adeline’s expression shifted from polite interest to absolute exhaustion. She’d been putting on a brave face for the customer, but it looked like she’d deserved every one of those bless-your-hearts.

“Hi,” I said hesitantly as I walked up to the counter.

“Hazel.” Adeline nodded at me solemnly. “Let’s go to my office.” She called out a name, and a man in his twenties appeared from one of the aisles. “I’ve got a meeting, so I’ll be in the back.”

I followed Adeline to her small office at the rear of the shop. There was a high window in the small room, and I knew there was a trashcan beneath it in the alley outside. I had stood next to it when I eavesdropped on Adeline, hoping to get evidence she had murdered the man whose body had been found in my garage.

Instead, I had gotten a sore rear end from knocking myself flat on the ground when my magic backfired, and I’d been embarrassed when Adeline had run out the back door of the shop to find out what had caused such a commotion. I would never admit to her that I’d thought she was a murder suspect, especially now that she really was one.

Adeline shut the door to her office, then slid behind a small desk absolutely piled with papers and manila file folders. A closed laptop sat in the middle of the chaos. “Sorry,” she said, gesturing at the desk. “I’m almost two hundred years old, and I still do a lot of our ordering and inventory the old-fashioned way.”

"I keep a hand-written calendar for my delivery service," I told her. "I'm not too modern, either." I sat down in one of the two chairs on the other side of the desk, my eyes darting around to avoid looking into Adeline's intense gaze.

"You heard my last conversation with Vincent," Adeline said.

That got me to look at her. *Is this why she called me?* "The one where you warned him that there are laws governing what witches can and can't do?"

"That's the one. Even though there's no security camera footage from the night of the murder, I reviewed footage from the couple of days prior to see if I spotted anything suspicious. I didn't, unfortunately, but I did see that you and one other customer were inside the store when Vincent and I had that talk."

"I assume you've reached out to that person, as well?"

"No. What's the point? You're the one who solves murders."

Oh. Well. I felt both complimented and a tad taken aback. Was that really my reputation? "How could my overhearing your conversation with Vincent help you prove your innocence? The security camera should have caught the conversation, too."

"The camera only records video, not audio." Adeline paused, and she brought both hands together on the desk, her fingers lacing tightly. "The constables suspect me of killing Vincent, of course."

"Because it happened in your store?"

"No. Because of our history."

My mouth dropped open, and I quickly shut it. "You two didn't get along?" I asked.

Adeline snorted. "That's an understatement. Vincent moved to this town about seven years ago, and he was a problem for me from day one. Vampires haven't always been able to live side-by-side with other supernatural creatures, and certainly not with humans. There was a time when we were considered monsters."

I thought of the rumors about a hunter being in town, and I nodded. "Vampires were once shunned."

"And one of the reasons we were shunned was because of unethical vampires like Vincent." Adeline gazed at an ancient-looking tapestry hanging on one wall. It depicted a woman leading a unicorn through a forest. "We can mesmerize. You know, hold people in our gaze and bend them to do our will. Except, these days, there are laws about mesmerizing, just like there are laws about magic."

"I'm guessing Vincent didn't like following the rules for either."

"That's right. He owned his own advertising business, working with clients here and down in Stanton. Vincent would sometimes mesmerize business owners to get them to run ads they didn't really want or need, so he'd get a paycheck for designing them. I figured it out when he started using witchcraft to help him amplify his power. The items he was buying here were clearly for magical influence over others."

"I take it your last conversation about it with him was far from the first."

Adeline laughed darkly. "I've been very vocal about my feelings toward him and his unethical practices."

"I'm glad to know this, because it solves one riddle for me. I first saw Vincent on Tuesday night, when he came into the tavern and got into a fight with a werewolf named Connor. The fight was because Connor was accusing Vincent of shady stuff. Now I know what that shady stuff was."

"I heard all about that fight. If you ask me, Vincent deserved it. Who knows how many non-magical people he mesmerized around Stanton, and they'll never even realize it."

"This is all interesting information," I assured Adeline, "but I still don't understand how you think I can help you."

"You heard our last conversation. You know I was warning him, not threatening him. Sure, I kicked him out of my shop, but my anger wasn't out of control. The constables will be talking to you at some point, because you're a witness."

"I was not at all concerned for Vincent's safety when I overheard your conversation with him," I assured Adeline. "And I'll reiterate that to the constables when they come asking for information."

Adeline had started to relax during our conversation, but she stiffened again. "Plus, I'm hoping you'll keep my innocence in mind while you're eavesdropping and tripping over clues around town."

I could have been offended by those words, but instead, I burst out laughing. "I'll do what I can."

"Thanks." Adeline stood up. Our meeting was clearly over. I wished her a good night and left, and I walked very slowly back to the tavern, because I wanted time to process everything Adeline had told me. Vincent had been mesmerizing non-magical people, and he'd been using magic to boost his power to control people's minds.

If people like Adeline and Connor really had been spreading the word about Vincent's shady dealings, then there was no telling who might have decided he had to be stopped. Not only had Vincent been breaking the law, but he'd also stepped across a huge ethical line, and he'd done it outside the magical community. It was bad enough to think of Vincent using magic and mesmerizing against people in Foxfire Haven, but if his manipulation had come to light in Stanton, it would have exposed the supernatural world.

But, no matter how long the suspect list was, I wasn't taking Adeline's name off of it just because she was proclaiming her innocence. As she had said, vampires were once shut out from society, and she wouldn't have wanted Vincent doing anything that might force vampires back into the shadows.

I was still a hundred feet away from the tavern when two men stumbled out the door and onto the sidewalk. One seemed to be struggling to hold the other up. The man who couldn't keep his feet under him was Harris, who was obviously drunk. The man helping him was Roscoe, my uncle's former best friend and one of the meanest old men in town. As I watched, Roscoe poured Harris into the side of a pickup truck parked on the curb, then walked around to the driver's side.

"Huh," I said to myself. "He can actually be nice."

What was even nicer was knowing Valerian no longer needed us to watch over her. She could finish up her shift in peace, and the rest of us could breathe a bit easier.

I got inside the tavern only to see Valerian coming around the end of the bar. "I'm free," she stated. "It's not busy enough that I need to stay and help our nighttime bartender."

"We're meeting Jo at The Salt Circle," Marlee informed me as she sailed past. "Val is buying us dinner!"

"It's the least I can do for my security team," Valerian said, giving me a lopsided smile.

Before long, all four of us were settled into a booth at The Salt Circle Cafe. We had been lucky to grab the last one available. Jo had come directly from the newspaper office, and she was yawning as she sat down. Hearing details about my meeting with Adeline perked her right up, though.

"This is going to be a huge story when it gets out," Jo said eagerly. "Mesmerizing and magic? Both used on people who don't even know the supernatural world exists?" She gave a low whistle.

I felt a gentle tap against my shoulder, and I glanced back to see the woman in the booth behind looking at me with wide eyes.

I know those eyes. It took me a second to realize it was Shawna, whom I'd delivered food to just the day before. "Sonny Dawes told me he was out in his field early yesterday morning, and he saw three men come out of the line of trees. He'd never seen them before, and when he called to them, they ran back into the woods."

"Who do you think they were?" I asked.

"Hunters, obviously. There's not just one up in this part of the country. There are three of them, right here in Foxfire Haven. And I'll bet you Vincent's behavior is what brought them here."

Chapter Thirteen

"Hunters?" A man walking past us stopped and spun to face Shawna. "Here?"

Shawna nodded at the man. "Three of them, right here in Foxfire Haven."

"In this day and age? Oh, dear. My wife, she's half-shifter. Is she in danger? What about our kids?" The man's high forehead broke out in a sweat, and he absently swiped a hand across it.

"Take precautions," Shawna told him calmly. "Be vigilant. And, don't forget, magic can help protect you. If we all face this together, we can run those hunters right out of town."

"Right. Together. Magic." The man walked away, talking to himself.

Our server, Sophie, soon stood in his place. She had a tray of dirty plates balanced in one hand. "Did I hear something about hunters? I heard that rumor that a hunter is in the area. I'd better warn Newton."

Newton Yates was a werefrog, and he was already the nervous type, perhaps even more so than the man Shawna had just sent off in a fit of muttering. I hated to think how Newton would react to this news.

"I don't buy it," Valerian said loudly, and we all turned to her.

"Why would Sonny make that up?" Shawna asked.

Valerian waved a hand. "Oh, I don't doubt Sonny saw some people, but what makes him so certain they were hunters? Maybe they took off because they were afraid Sonny would holler at them about trespassing. He does like to gripe at people, so I wouldn't blame anyone for running away from him."

"These weren't locals, though," Shawna countered. "I've got a dear friend who's a werewolf, and I'm worried for him."

"That I can understand," Valerian assured Shawna. "You told that man to be vigilant, and that's good advice, but it's important not to blow this rumor up into something larger than life."

"I'm just looking out for my friends," Shawna said sharply. She clearly didn't appreciate Valerian's skepticism, and she turned back around to continue her conversation with the others at her booth.

Jo, Marlee, Valerian, and I looked at each other silently, and slowly, each one of us gave a short nod. We didn't need to speak to know we were all thinking the same thing: Valerian was right that there was no need to give credence to vague rumors. Someone had murdered Vincent, but he'd made plenty of enemies around Foxfire Haven, so a hunter showing up to take him out seemed like the least likely scenario.

"Occam's Razor," I said under my breath.

"What's that?" Jo asked.

"Occam's Razor. You know, the idea that the simplest explanation is the likeliest one. In the span of a couple days, I saw Vincent clash with three different people. How many more folks around town did he also cause trouble for?"

Marlee picked up her fork and waved it in the air. "In other words, how many suspects do we have from right here in our own community? I'm guessing a lot."

"And it's most likely one of those suspects who's responsible for Vincent's death, rather than a hunter," Valerian finished for her.

"You three get it," I said. The rumor that a hunter had been spotted in the Pacific Northwest was ridiculous enough, but three of them in our town seemed downright impossible.

Unfortunately, the rest of the patrons and staff at The Salt Circle didn't seem to agree with us. A few minutes after ordering our food, I heard a woman's raised voice coming from somewhere nearby. "Hunters! We're in danger!"

Across the aisle, a man called someone on his cell phone, and I heard him say, "Ask Margaret to pull out her grimoire. You're going to need warding spells."

The volume in the cafe steadily rose as the news about the three hunters—the *alleged* three hunters—spread like wildfire. Valerian shook her head. "I'm glad I'm not working tonight. It's going to be nothing but hunter talk at the tavern."

"It's definitely a night to be at home, where there will be no gossip and no panic," I agreed.

That expectation lasted until about eight thirty that evening. Jo and Marlee were both in the living room, watching TV, while Valerian and I were in the dining room with a game of Scrabble between us. I had just laid down tiles spelling *suspect*, which seemed appropriate for the day, when there was a loud knock at the door.

"Probably Wyatt," Valerian said as I rose from my chair. We had all fallen into the assumption that if anyone showed up at our door early in the morning or late at night, it must be our neighbor the chief constable.

When I reached the main hallway, I saw that Jo had moved faster than me. As she turned the doorknob, a screech echoed down the hallway. It almost sounded like a scream.

Jo froze, her hand on the doorknob, as she turned and gazed around the hallway. "Who screamed?"

"I don't think it was a person making that sound," I said.

Marlee came flying out of the living room. "I just felt a spike of emotion. Someone is anxious and worried, like danger is on the horizon."

"Or at the door," Valerian said. She had followed me out of the dining room.

Jo slowly uncurled her fingers from the doorknob, right as the knocking sounded again. She stepped back and raised her hands, as if to assure us she wasn't going to open the door. "Who is it?" she called loudly.

"It's Harris" came the voice from the other side of the door.

"What do you want?"

"I'm here to check on Val. There are hunters in town!"

Jo leaned so she could look past me. "Val?" she whispered.

Valerian shook her head so hard her braid whipped through the air behind her. Although she looked worried and annoyed, Jo began to smile, and she winked at Valerian.

"Sorry, Harris," Jo called. "We're all locked in for the night. We have to take precautions to stay safe from those hunters."

"But I'm not a hunter! I'm here to help keep you all safe."

"It's okay. Our poltergeist has things under control." Jo was grinning now, and I saw her shoulders shake with silent laughter.

"Oh. Is the ghost...on watch?" Harris sounded nervous.

"Yes, and only the four of us are allowed inside the house."

"I see. Okay. I'll go, then." By the sound of it, Harris was already leaving. I heard footsteps, and his voice was less clear.

After a moment, we all heard the slam of a car door, followed by an engine rumbling to life.

All four of us began to laugh.

"Jo," Valerian said, wiping at one eye, "that was absolutely brilliant! You turned his lame excuse for coming here against him!"

"And I love that the threat of the poltergeist was enough to get him to leave!" Marlee pressed a hand to her chest. "The threat was legitimate, I think. I expect the ghost was the one warning us that there was danger at the door."

"Smart ghost," Valerian said.

I had two deliveries scheduled for the next morning, with the first one at eight o'clock. When I began to put on my coat, I was surprised to see Perkins fluttering toward me. I had already fed him and given him plenty of gentle strokes on his tiny head, and I had left him snuggled deep in his flannel nest.

"What is it, Perky?" I asked as I buttoned my coat.

In answer, Perkins landed on my shoulder and scooted close to my neck.

"Do you want to come with me today?"

A soft coo was, I figured, a yes. Perkins was usually content to stay at home when I was out and about, so his eagerness to come with me was unusual. I wondered if the poltergeist had him feeling jumpy, or if he was simply ready for a change in scenery.

Inside the hearse, I used my scarf to make a cozy little nest on the floor of the passenger side. Perkins settled into it, and before long, he and I were on our way to Stacy's Stationery and Sundries. I was nervous about going there again, but I told myself that if Stacy had lost all faith in my ability to safely be around her products, then she would have canceled the appointment.

The shop was free of self-warming teacups when I walked inside. A sign on one of the empty shelves read *Something new coming soon!*

"Good morning," I called, even though I couldn't see anyone. Perkins, who was perched on my shoulder again, hooted loudly.

"Over here." Stacy's voice came from somewhere near the back of the store. I found her sitting on the floor in front of a display of fountain pens, where she was placing pens, inkwells, and price signs in a neat arrangement.

I decided to dive right into the topic that had me feeling nervous. "Any word on the teacup bill?"

Stacy grinned up at me. "You don't owe me a dime."

I should have been delighted by that news, but instead, I was confused. "I don't understand."

"I called and talked to the person who makes those teacups. As it turns out, his girlfriend cursed that batch of teacups as revenge for not remembering her birthday. He found out, and, of course, there are magical laws against that kind of thing. She has to pay for all the damages, both to the teacups and my store."

"Hopefully, he broke up with her, too," I said. *What a petty person she must be,* I thought. She could have hurt someone if they had been sipping tea from one of the cursed cups when it began to act up.

"Oh, yeah. I'd call that a red flag, for sure. Anyway, the person responsible for the curse is responsible for all the teacups, regardless of the fact that you came along and shattered them. In fact, if you hadn't broken the teacups, they might have caused even more damage to the shop. Apparently, one of the cursed cups got sold to a witch in New Hampshire, and she wasn't home when the teacup began to malfunction. It heated up so much it started a fire inside her kitchen cabinet. She got home just in time to put it out with the fire extinguisher before it spread."

"Yikes. I'm glad to hear I inadvertently helped, but I want you to know I'm still working hard at controlling my magic."

"I know you are. Anyway, today's job involves nothing breakable, so you should be just fine. I've got five boxes of spring-themed stationery at my warehouse." Quickly, Stacy gave me the details, and soon enough, Perkins and I were on our way to pick up the stationery.

After I returned with the boxes, Stacy and I were stacking them in the back storage room when she said, "Have you heard about the three hunters in town? Sonny Dawes spotted them!"

"I've heard that rumor."

"I'm going to have a flash sale on my inks with protection spells on them. The vampires and shifters in town can use them to write their warding incantations."

"That's a good idea." I wished Stacy good luck with the sale, then left to head to my next delivery appointment. When I pulled up in front of the bookstore, I paused to text Jo before getting out of the hearse. *You should give Barry a heads up about the hunter rumors*, I typed. *Just in case.*

Stacy had mentioned vampires and shifters being wary, but they weren't the only supernatural creatures who would be vulnerable to a hunter attack.

After I had shuttled some books for out-of-town customers to the post office, I went to the magic store to pick up a few things for a warding spell Val had mentioned that morning during coffee. None of us had the carnelian required for it, so I had volunteered to swing by Into the Cauldron for it. Perkins had fallen asleep, curled up in my scarf, so I cracked open a window and left him in the hearse.

I felt a bit of trepidation going into the crystal aisle, because I half expected to see that pile of ash again. Of course, that wasn't the case. There was no indication a vampire had been murdered on that spot.

However, as I was trying to decide which piece of carnelian I wanted to buy, I noticed a piece of paper at the back of the shelf. It was about the size of an envelope, and it was folded in half. I was just reaching out to grab it, when I heard a man's voice directly behind me shout, "Don't!"

I was so startled my adrenaline shot up, which, in turn, built my magic up to a critical level in a heartbeat.

I was about to blow up the entire crystal aisle.

Chapter Fourteen

"HAZEL, TRY TO HOLD on." This time, I recognized the voice. I also recognized the edge of panic in it.

"Wyatt," I said breathlessly. It was all I could get out because I was concentrating so hard on not letting my magic escape me.

I felt Wyatt's hands curl around my shoulders. When he spoke again, his lips were close to my ear, and his voice was soft and calm, almost monotone. "You are safe. You are in control. Your magic obeys your will."

Mentally, I began to recite my usual calming spell. Once I felt like I had stepped back from the brink of an immediate magical exhalation, I whispered the incantation again. As I did so, Wyatt gently steered me by the shoulders. My eyes were squeezed shut as I focused on the spell, so I trusted him to guide me safely outside, where I knew he was taking me.

When Wyatt stopped me and dropped his hold on my shoulders, I opened my eyes to see the door in front of me. I pushed it open and stepped out onto the sidewalk. The cold air against my face felt invigorating, and I repeated the calming spell again.

Then, I switched to the spell for shedding my magic. Usually, I preferred to do it with no one watching because it felt so personal. Shameful, really. I was ashamed I had to shed my magic so often, and I didn't want anyone to see me doing it.

At that moment, though, I was far more worried about causing damage to the magic store than I was about bruising my ego. My pink magic was soon pooled at my feet, the sparkles glinting in the sunshine.

"I'm sorry," Wyatt said suddenly.

I turned to him wordlessly, and he dropped his head. "I should have known better than to surprise you like that."

"Because I'm dangerous," I said. Wyatt didn't have to say anything. I knew from the way his eyebrows drew together that I had just finished his thought. "You startled me in there. I hadn't heard you walk up, and suddenly, someone was yelling at me. Why didn't you want me to grab that piece of paper?"

Wyatt shrugged. "It could be evidence. I came here to walk along that aisle again, hoping I might find something we'd missed the first time. You found it first."

"You know me, always drawing clues to myself," I said sarcastically.

Wyatt shook his head, and his eyes crinkled with amusement. "Someday, you'll believe me about that."

"Thanks for keeping me calm," I said. "Even though it was your fault I almost destroyed the store."

"And here I was just thinking that you and I were finally starting to get along with each other."

"I'll call a truce if you let me come with you to see what that paper is."

Wyatt gazed at me thoughtfully, as if he were weighing up how dangerous it would be to let me accompany him. Eventually, he said, "Okay, but at the first sign of trouble, you are out."

"Agreed."

I stayed several steps behind Wyatt as I followed him inside. Soon, we were standing in front of the carnelian display again. I still had to pick one and purchase it, but first, I wanted to know if that piece of paper was evidence of some kind.

And, if it was, how had the constables missed it the first time around?

Wyatt took several photos of the paper with his phone, then pulled out a multi-tool. It looked like a pocketknife on steroids, with at least twenty different tools tucked into it. Wyatt levered out tiny tweezers and used them to gingerly lift the paper. He moved some crystals out of the way so he could lay it down and unfold it, still using the tweezers to avoid getting his own fingerprints on it.

"*Mother-of-pearl, eyebright, silver-toned silk, citrine,*" he read. "Someone dropped their shopping list."

I repeated the items to myself. "It might have been Vincent's shopping list," I concluded. "Those things are all used for psychic power. And if Vincent was working magic to boost his mesmerizing ability, these items could have been used in a spell for psychic mastery."

"Ms. Beaumont mentioned Vincent's magical mesmerizing tactics." Wyatt looked around. "There has to be a spare bag around here I can put this in."

I volunteered to ask for one at the cash register, and when I came back with one in hand, Wyatt carefully slid the paper inside it. "How did we miss this the first time?" he asked, more to himself than to me.

"I wondered the same thing," I admitted. I thought of Adeline's request, and I said, "I was in here the day Vincent got kicked out."

"Ms. Beaumont told me. She said you and one other customer had likely overheard her discussion with Vincent."

"Then why haven't you asked me for my account of it?"

Wyatt lifted a shoulder in a shrug. "If you had thought the conversation was worth telling me about, you would have."

He might not trust my magic, but he trusts my judgment. I reached up to push my hair behind my ear, and I remembered how close Wyatt had been to me when he was helping me maintain my control. It was the second time in only a few days we had been in physical contact like that, and both times, it was because of my magic.

A sensation that felt similar to goosebumps broke out on my arms and shoulders. Except, the feeling wasn't on the outside of my skin. It was inside. Despite the shedding spell, my magic was on the rise again.

"Good point. I should let you wrap up here." My words were tumbling out in my haste. "Have a good day."

I turned and hustled down the aisle and out the door. Behind me, I thought I heard Wyatt ask, "What did I do?" but I couldn't risk stopping to explain. As soon as my feet hit the sidewalk, I stopped and did another shedding spell, despite the fact there were people walking past. And, even if I had answered Wyatt, I don't know what

I would have said. Sometimes, it seemed like just being around him made my magic spike.

It was only after I had climbed behind the wheel of the hearse that I realized I hadn't bought that carnelian for the spell that night, but there was absolutely no way I was going back inside while Wyatt was in there. I would head back later, or I could ask one of the other members of my coven to go.

When Perkins and I got home, I found Valerian at the kitchen table. There were shot glasses, a mortar and pestle, and a few small bowls in front of her, and she was carefully pouring a lime-green liquid into a pint glass. The shimmering liquid was in a beaker, and that along with the look of excitement in her eyes gave her mad-scientist vibes.

"Working on a new potion?" I asked.

"I need something to get Harris off my back."

"Careful, Val," I said, thinking of the story Stacy had told me that morning. "You don't want to risk breaking any laws about working dark magic against others."

Valerian finished pouring the liquid and set the beaker down. "This isn't dark magic. And I'm not going to lie when I tell Harris what it is. It's a Put Your Best Foot Forward potion."

"You think he'll misinterpret its purpose," I guessed.

"It's designed to help the drinker be less negative toward others," Valerian explained. "I think Harris will understand that, and he'll drink it as a show that he wants to avoid getting into another fight when he's at the tavern. Of course, his behavior toward me is negative, so while this potion might not get rid of him, it should make him act less creepy."

I poured myself a glass of water and sat down to watch Valerian work. She carefully spooned some kind of powdered herb into the glass she was using to mix ingredients, then glanced up at me. "You look worn out."

"I ran into Wyatt at Into the Cauldron and almost blew him up. Again."

"He sure seems to get you worked up."

I let out a short laugh. "And, this time, he even admitted it was his fault that my magic spiked."

After I told Valerian about the encounter, she gave me a sly look. "You forgot something. You just had a run-in with Wyatt, but you haven't once mentioned what a grump he is."

"He was...pretty nice. He wasn't a curmudgeon, at least."

"Mm-hmm."

I felt warmth in my cheeks. "I do not have a thing for Wyatt. I don't like him, remember?"

"Sure, sure." Valerian was still smiling to herself as she lifted a bowl filled with a shimmery purple powder.

I was saved from having to continue the conversation by my phone ringing. As I pulled it out of my purse to answer, I silently thanked whomever was on the other end.

The caller was Millie, who owned Back to Realitea. The sweet little tea shop had become a favorite spot of mine, and Millie had recently hired me to help with some of her deliveries. This time, she was asking if I had time to run to the restaurant supply store in Stanton.

"I have a huge group in here, and another coming tonight for a private party, and my scones are nearly gone!" Millie said in her light British accent. "I need flour and butter to keep up with demand!"

After reassuring her that I was happy to drop everything and make the run, Millie told me exactly what she needed and how much of it while I carefully wrote everything down.

Ninety minutes later, I was walking inside Back to Realitea with two heavy shopping bags in my hands. Millie thanked me profusely as I handed them over, and even her black-and-white cat came over to rub against my legs in what felt like a show of gratitude. I turned to go, but as I did, I caught sight of the witch who had been so disgruntled with Adeline that she had been working magic against her.

Her back was to me, so I called out to the mass of fluffy brown hair. "Natalie?"

Natalie turned toward me, and she looked confused for a moment. Then, she chuckled. "You and I keep running into each other!" She carefully put her teacup down on its saucer and swiveled in her chair to get a better look at me. Her purple blouse clashed with the mint-green tablecloths and floral wallpaper, and I realized she was sitting with two other women that I'd seen her with at the tavern. They were giving me looks of distrust.

"I guess your spell worked," I said. "Adeline says the constables think she might have killed Vincent."

Natalie's face broke into a wide smile. "I know. The last time I saw that man, he was walking into her store, and I had a gut feeling he'd be the one to help me bring down Adeline. Call it a witch's intuition. I just didn't know at the time that he'd do it by getting himself staked in the crystal aisle."

I fought to keep my expression neutral as I realized with a start that Natalie had been in the magic store at nearly the same time Vincent had been killed. She'd even told me she was on the way there that day, and I'd forgotten about it until that moment.

I had been making a list of suspects based on who had a grudge against Vincent. Now, I wondered if he'd been killed to make Adeline look guilty.

Chapter Fifteen

Surely, I told myself, Natalie wouldn't be bragging about her magic against Adeline if she had been the one to kill Vincent.

Or, maybe, that was the point. The more she crowed about her success, the less anyone would consider her a suspect.

One of the other women at the table cleared their throat loudly, and I blinked rapidly as the sound pulled me out of my thoughts. I gave Natalie a tight smile. "Have a good day."

As I turned to go, though, she called, "Wait. It's Hazel, right?" When I nodded, she continued, "Tell your coven to be on the lookout. There's a rumor that three hunters have been spotted in town, and even though we witches are probably safe, it's best if we're all on alert."

Is Natalie saying that to make me think a hunter killed Vincent? Is she trying to make herself look innocent?

Whatever the truth was, I smiled again. It probably looked fake, but it was the best I could do. "I've heard the same rumor. I hope you ladies don't have any run-ins."

I didn't drive home after that. Instead, I drove to the constable station. It was close enough to the tea shop that I could have walked, but if I had done that, I would have risked running into Natalie again when I came back for the hearse.

The Foxfire Haven Constables had a long one-story building on the edge of downtown, and it was one of the few buildings in that area that felt decidedly non-magical. Most places had an air of the supernatural, whether it was the atmosphere, the decor, or the people inside. Like the post office and the DMV, the constable station was straightforward and utilitarian.

When I walked inside, I saw the front desk directly across from me, which was manned by a bored-looking constable who was doodling in a notebook. She barely looked up as I walked in. "How can I help you?"

"Hi. I'm here to see Chief Constable Hightower."

"He's out."

"Do you know when he'll be back?"

"No." The woman paused, then added, "Do you want to leave a message?" She patted a sheet of paper to her right, which had a list of names and phone numbers on it.

"Are those all for him?"

"Yep."

Poor Wyatt. I knew he worked hard and had a lot of responsibility, but I couldn't imagine how it would feel to get back to the office and find a huge list of people demanding his time and attention. I wanted to tell him about Natalie, but I didn't want to add to his stress. I'd given him enough of that with my crisis at Into the Cauldron.

Suddenly, and to my utter surprise, I started to giggle. The constable stared up at me like I had a third ear growing out of my forehead, and I clamped my teeth together in an attempt to recover my composure. "Sorry. I was just thinking of something, um, funny. I'll try getting in touch with the chief constable later."

I left the constable station, no longer giggling but feeling a growing sense of realization. Valerian had been right. I liked Wyatt. Otherwise, why would I care how long his list of messages was or how late he might have to work that night?

And why would I care that I had caused him trouble?

I thought about Wyatt the entire drive home, and I was so distracted I nearly grazed the edge of the garage door as I guided the hearse inside for the night.

Marlee was filling Valerian in on a meeting she'd had with a client as I walked into the kitchen. The two of them both looked me up and down. "You okay?" Valerian asked.

Before I could answer, Marlee said, "You're confused about something."

Yeah, my feelings about Wyatt. That, though, wasn't something I was ready to admit. Before I said anything about it to my coven, I needed to figure out what, exactly, those feelings were. I told myself firmly it wasn't anything romantic, and that Wyatt and I were finally becoming friends. That was it.

"I think a witch named Natalie might have killed Vincent and framed Adeline for it," I said.

"Natalie," Valerian repeated. "She's the one who blames Adeline for a spell that went wrong. She loves to badmouth the woman, but I don't know that she would frame her for murder."

"She's also been working magic against Adeline," I pointed out.

Marlee made a noise of disapproval. "Dangerous. And mean."

I sighed. "The next time I talk to Hailey, I'm going to reiterate the importance of being a nice witch."

"How was your latest lesson with her?" Valerian asked.

"Chaotic." I smiled and shook my head at the memory. My four-year-old granddaughter would be a powerful witch when she grew up, but at her young age, learning to control her magic was proving to be a challenge. I could relate, and I loved having my weekly video calls with her so we could talk about how to feel magic and how to keep it from becoming too strong. Teaching Hailey, I had realized, was a good reminder for myself, too.

"If there really is an energy source here that's feeding our magic," Marlee said, "it's probably not a good idea for Hailey to be around it."

"Good thing my daughter and her family live in San Francisco, then."

Marlee's forehead creased as she gave me a look of sympathy.

My heart sank as I realized why Marlee was giving me that look. "Oh, right. Tara and I were making plans for them to visit again in late spring."

"All the more reason for us to track down this energy source and get it under control," Valerian said firmly. "But back to Natalie. Do you really think she might have framed Adeline for Vincent's murder? And if so, have you told Wyatt your hunch yet?"

"Yes, I think it's possible, and no, I haven't told Wyatt. I stopped by the constable station on my way home, but he was out. I'll text him later. In the meantime, I'm going to unwind with a book and try not to think about the murder, or magic, or anything else."

Soon, I was curled up on the sofa in the living room, a flannel blanket tucked around me and Perkins settled on my lap. Stella, who had become something like a best friend to Perkins, had followed us. She had used her long orange beak to curl a corner of the blanket around herself, and all I could see were a few black toucan tail feathers sticking out from the edge of the blanket.

Maybe it was everything I had experienced that day, or maybe it was watching the two birds snoozing happily, but I only read a few pages before I felt my eyes beginning to droop. I decided to close them for a minute or two, and when I opened them again, I felt groggy.

I glanced at my watch and saw it was after seven o'clock. I had conked out.

I heard Jo's distinctive footsteps out in the hallway, followed by the sound of the doorbell. "Coming!" she called.

Our visitor must have rung once already, and I guessed that was what had woken me up. Gently, I moved Perkins off my lap and onto the sofa. Stella was nowhere to be found, and I figured she had gone in search of Marlee while I had been napping.

I stood and stretched while my neck protested about the angle it had been at during my snooze. I figured whoever was at the door wasn't there for me, so I headed for the kitchen in search of a glass of water as I heard Jo open the door and say, "Oh, hello! I'm so glad you're here. Come on in."

Marlee and Valerian were working on dinner when I came into the kitchen. I yawned, then said, "Jo has a visitor."

"Oh, is it someone for her?" Marlee dropped diced garlic into the pot of pasta sauce on the stove. "I guess the doorbell woke you up. You're lucky, because Jo was threatening to have Gordon sit on your head until you stirred."

I rubbed my neck. "Then I would hurt even more." I poured myself a glass of water, then added, "How can I help?"

Valerian opened her mouth to answer, but just then, there were footsteps followed by Jo asking, "Do we have enough for one more?"

I was surprised to see it was Wyatt following Jo through the doorway. He shook his head. "I told you, Josephine, I'm happy to make myself something at home."

"Nonsense," Valerian said. "We've got plenty, and you've had a long day of keeping the people of Foxfire Haven in line." I noticed the pointed glance Valerian sent my way, but I wasn't sure if Wyatt had noticed it.

"I only had to keep one person in line, so it wasn't too bad of a day." Wyatt's eyes were sparkling as he looked at me. Yes, he had definitely understood Valerian's implication that I was the reason he'd had a long day.

"At least my name wasn't on your messages list." I opened the cabinet and began to pull five plates out of it while Jo moved an extra chair to the kitchen table.

"I stopped by the constable station to talk to you, but there were a lot of people who got there before me, apparently."

"Most of them can wait until tomorrow, and two of them are people who call regularly with wild conspiracies that aren't worth my time." Wyatt sat down at the table and stretched his long legs out in front of him. "Lately, it's been people telling me they saw someone they didn't recognize, and therefore, that person must be one of the alleged hunters in town."

"Hazel has a tip for you that has nothing to do with hunters," Valerian said as she put a glass filled with a blue liquid in front of Wyatt. "Here, it's got chamomile and vervain in it. It will help you wind down."

"Thanks." Wyatt sounded slightly uncomfortable, like he wasn't used to being fussed over. I didn't know why he'd come to our door, but he clearly hadn't counted on being served dinner and a potion.

"What brings you here?" I asked.

"You." Wyatt took a long sip of the potion, then hummed in satisfaction. "Outstanding, Valerian."

"Me?" I asked. "What did I do?" It was the same question Wyatt had asked me as I'd made my hasty exit from Into the Cauldron earlier.

"You stopped by the station to see me."

"Yes, but how did you know? I only told you just now."

Wyatt laughed. "Hazel, you underestimate how well-known you are in this town. You didn't leave a message, but when Constable Donner handed me the list, she also told me you'd stopped in. Then, three other constables mentioned they saw either you or your hearse."

"I guess I am a little conspicuous in that thing. Like Val said, I have a tip for you. I think it's possible someone killed Vincent in an attempt to frame Adeline. And that someone is a witch named Natalie."

Wyatt groaned. "Natalie Gil. She's one of the most vindictive people I've ever met."

"She did tell me she worked magic against Adeline. And, today, she mentioned being at Into the Cauldron at the same time as Vincent."

Wyatt sat up straight and quickly put his potion down. "The night he was staked?"

I nodded, and Wyatt chewed his lip thoughtfully for a moment. "I'll have a talk with her tomorrow. It's so frustrating when a vampire dies like this. I can't talk to the body, because there's no body to talk to."

Marlee and I exchanged a confused look, and Valerian said, "Dead people don't talk back, anyway."

"They do to me." Wyatt sighed. "I'm a necromancer."

Chapter Sixteen

"I'd always assumed you were a witch," Valerian said. She had frozen in the middle of chopping broccoli, and her fingers were white as she gripped the knife.

Is Val afraid of Wyatt because he's a necromancer?

"I knew," Jo said. "It's been mentioned in several newspaper articles over the years, though most were stories I came across during research. I've never written about your magical ability for a story."

"It's been a while since I've put it to use," Wyatt said.

"But why?" I asked. "There have been multiple murders since I moved back here, and you're telling me you could have simply had a conversation with each victim to find out who killed them?"

"There's nothing simple about it," Wyatt countered. His eyebrows drew down, and he sat up stiffly.

"I understand a victim might not know who killed them, but talking to them should at least help you get a good idea who your suspects are."

"Necromancy is a difficult art, and having a conversation with the dead isn't always possible."

I could tell Wyatt was clenching his jaw. After how well we had been getting along lately, we were on the verge of a blowup. Necromancers were incredibly rare, and Wyatt should have been proud of his ability. Instead, he seemed defensive about it.

And, I knew, the best thing I could do in that moment was to shut my mouth.

The silence was broken by Valerian, who finally put the knife down. "You can bring the dead back to life?"

"No," Wyatt said quickly. "That's dark magic, and we've all heard stories about the pitfalls of raising the dead. No one ever comes back like they should. I use my magic to have a last conversation with the dead, helping them recall the final impressions they had during life. If a body is too old, it's impossible. With vampires, there isn't even a body to talk to."

Valerian visibly relaxed. "That I can deal with. You're almost like a psychic medium, except you're talking to bodies instead of ghosts."

"Don't worry, Valerian. I'm not raising zombies or anything nefarious like that." Wyatt gave us all a look that was teasing, but I could still sense his anger in the glint of his eyes. "I'm not that bad."

"Drink your potion," Marlee insisted, "and let's talk about something happier."

Wyatt obediently took another sip of his drink, and he slowly began to settle back into his chair.

"This may not be a happier subject," I said carefully, "but we think we've figured out why my magic keeps spiraling out of control."

"Not your magic," Marlee corrected me. "*Our* magic. It's increasing for all four of us."

Wyatt looked around the table. "How so?"

"My manifesting is working a little too well," Jo said. "I haven't even told anyone about what happened today. A few days ago, I wrote an intention that I'd have something exciting happen soon. Well, last night, I woke up to the sound of the hangers in my closet clacking together. I turned on the light right as all my clothes fell to the floor."

"And that's the other thing," I said. "The poltergeist's power is growing, too."

"And Holman's," Marlee pointed out.

"Something is acting like a magical battery," Wyatt guessed.

All four of us nodded.

"We think there's some kind of energy source here on the property," I explained. "An energy well, or a vortex of some kind. My theory is that Uncle Grant learned about it, and that's what he was searching for in his final years."

"That makes sense," Wyatt said. He folded his hands on top of the table and stared down into his empty glass. "I was here for a number of funerals during Grant's tenure as the director. Almost every time, the dead would speak to me, without my initiating it. It was like my magic was so strong that I didn't have to go through any of the usual incantations. Each time it happened, it would be stronger than the previous occasion: the dead would speak more clearly, and for a longer period of time."

"What would they say to you?" Valerian asked. She briskly rubbed her arms, like she'd gotten a chill.

"They'd describe their final moments or ask me to pass on a message to loved ones. Those who die peacefully don't tend to have a lot to say."

"So, anyone who's here for a long enough time gets a boost to their magic," I said slowly. "The four of us—"

"And the ghosts!" Marlee added.

"Yes, and probably our familiars, too, are getting the most from this energy well, but anyone who visits might get a bit of extra power, at least temporarily."

"Which means we don't want Harris or any other creeps trespassing here." Valerian smiled wryly. "But we'll be strong enough to put up a warding spell no one will want to challenge."

"Remind me to stay on your good side," Wyatt said.

"You have to get on our good side first, if you want to stay on it." To prove I was teasing, I gave Wyatt a wink. It was only after I'd done it that I realized how flirtatious it might have seemed.

I was saved from my embarrassment by Jo, who announced dinner was ready. Wyatt, again, tried to get out of staying, but Jo absolutely insisted that he stay with us. Jo and Marlee kept the conversation going while we ate, which I was grateful for. I was preoccupied with my conflicting feelings about Wyatt.

Stop it, I told myself. *If you keep dwelling on him, your magic will spike, and dinner will wind up all over the walls.*

Wyatt thanked us heartily once we'd finished dinner, and after he left, I breathed a sigh of relief. "What a night," I said as I loaded plates into the dishwasher.

"A necromancer," Valerian said. "I had no idea. I've always been terrified of their power."

"Wyatt *is* terrifying," I agreed.

"He didn't like talking about it," Marlee said. She threw a couple of cans into the recycling bin, then turned to us. "He's hiding something."

"But him being a necromancer is no secret." Jo shook her head. "He used his magic to solve a murder case about twenty years ago, and it's what helped put him on the path to being chief constable. His ability has been an enormous help to his career."

"Maybe that's why he's uncomfortable talking about it," Marlee speculated. "We all use our magic in our careers, to some extent, but maybe Wyatt feels like he got an unfair advantage. Or, perhaps, he's been made to feel that way by others."

I made a noise of content. "Whatever the truth is, I'm still amazed we all just ate dinner with Wyatt, and he and I didn't end the night in an argument. We're making progress."

"How sweet that you and your boyfriend are getting along better," Marlee teased.

I threw a dishtowel at her head.

Since I had a few quiet hours on Sunday morning, I took the shoebox full of Uncle Grant's photos and sat down with them at the dining room table. Perkins came along with me, sitting on the table near my elbow and cooing encouragingly.

The photos had already been sorted into chronological order, and I laid the first twenty or so onto the table. The last time I did that, I had been looking for more ghosts or some kind of pattern. This time, I tried to find what was different.

After ten minutes of staring, I hadn't found any kind of anomaly. To me, it just looked like the chronicles of a funeral director who was proud of the two beautiful chapels and other public spaces of the funeral home.

I gathered up those photos and laid out another batch. Again, I found nothing out of the ordinary.

What had Uncle Grant been trying to document? And why couldn't I figure it out?

I was on the fifth batch of photos, and rapidly getting to the bottom of the shoebox, when Perkins hopped to one photo, leaned forward, and gently pressed his beak against it.

"What?" I leaned closer to see what he was indicating. The photo was clearly of the back hallway, where the wallpaper was less flashy and there was no dark-wood wainscoting on the walls. Uncle Grant had been standing somewhere near the embalming room, which was currently Jo's bedroom, and he had aimed his camera in the direction of the kitchen door.

"It's just the back hall," I told Perkins. "No ghosts, no nothing."

In answer, Perkins gently tapped the photo again.

This time, I picked up the photo and held it close to my eyes. The spot Perkins had indicated was just a part of the wall, but he had noticed a sort of swirl in the faded green wallpaper. I squinted. It wasn't the wallpaper that was swirled, but something in front of it.

I'd seen photos of ghosts, including the one of the bearded man in the former casket showroom. Some ghosts, like that one, looked nearly corporeal. Others were more like a fine mist.

This swirl, though, wasn't like anything I had seen before.

"Is this energy?" I whispered. "Was Grant taking all these photos to try to capture it on film?"

Perkins elongated his neck once, like a reverse shrug. I figured it meant he didn't know the answer to my question.

"This could be energy flowing out of the source. Maybe it's inside the walls! Or underneath the house? Is it always in the same spot, or does it move around? How concentrated is it?"

I jumped up and ran into the hallway, not stopping until I was standing in front of the same spot pictured in the photo. It was just an ordinary wall.

If Uncle Grant was also trying to find this energy well, then it's no wonder he started acting strange. The questions and the uncertainty, coupled with the energy pouring into the house, could easily send someone over the edge in a frantic search for answers.

"I need fresh air," I announced to Perkins. "Let's go for a walk."

I grabbed my jacket, made sure Perkins was comfortably perched on my shoulder, then headed for the front door. I opened it just in time to see Shawna raising her hand to knock. She and I both jumped in surprise, then laughed.

"Wow, great timing!" Shawna said. Her smile disappeared. "The hunter problem is getting worse, and I'm going to need your coven's help if we're going to get them off our backs."

Chapter Seventeen

"Why do you need our help?" I asked bluntly.

Shawna reached up and tugged at one of her pigtails. "I am absolutely overwhelmed! Orders are pouring in from people wanting warding-spell kits and my other magical protection bundles. My assistants are working as hard as they can, but it's just a part-time job for all of them, so they only have so much time and energy to give me. So, I'm expanding! I'm hoping to hire your coven to help me fulfill orders."

Although I had been saved from paying for all the broken teacups at Stacy's Stationery and Sundries, I was still trying to get repairs made around the house, and I wanted to get my savings account back into a healthier state. And, I figured, there couldn't be any harm in hearing Shawna out. I invited her in, and soon, we were seated in the living room.

"Should I get Marlee and Val?" I asked. "I think both of them are in the kitchen."

"Nah. I've only got a couple of minutes, so I'll throw the idea out, and you can discuss it with them later." Shawna had sat down on the sofa, but she perched on the edge rather than settling in. "I'm on my way to deliver an order, and it occurred to me that your funeral home was just off my route, so I dove into your neighborhood for a quick hello. I'm as surprised by this visit as you are!"

"It was nice of you to stop by, though. You must think highly of our magic if you're looking for help from us."

Shawna laughed incredulously. "Think highly of your magic? Do you not know the reputation the funeral home coven has?"

I shook my head, wondering if word of my magical outbursts was sinking the reputation of my entire coven.

"Everyone in town knows about the incident at the tavern." Shawna pressed her lips together and gave me a significant look. I had no idea which incident she meant, since I had been involved in several there. When she realized my confusion, she clarified, "Your coven did a shielding spell when Melba Hawthorn was trying to curse everyone. I heard it was spectacular to watch."

A warm feeling of pride bloomed in my chest, and I sat up a little straighter. None of us were perfect, but we really were one incredible team. "I'm very lucky to be a part of this coven."

"You are, in part because of the opportunity I'm giving you to make some extra cash! I'm looking for help with preparing herb mixtures for my protection and warding spells, plus I need someone who can help refine some of my spell bundles that aren't quite strong enough yet. And, I especially need help delivering all these orders to customers around town. That's where you come in, of course. The rest of your coven can help with the other tasks."

Shawna went on to explain about how many hours per day she needed help, and she threw out an hourly rate that sounded decent. I promised to discuss everything with my coven, and she rose to go.

"Wait," I said as I stood and reached an arm toward her. "You said the hunter problem is getting worse. Did something happen?"

"You know Connor Ulmann?" Shawna shook her head and curled her hands tightly around the strap of her purse. "His son was playing in their front yard, and he spotted a man carrying a crossbow. No doubt it was fitted with an arrow made of silver."

"And they're a family of werewolves, so that's especially concerning for them." It was impossible for me to match Shawna's level of worry, since I was still unconvinced there was some kind of hunter invasion happening. Even Wyatt had passed it off as an alleged report rather than fact, and I was more inclined to believe him than a witch I barely knew. I thought it far more likely that Connor's son had heard the rumors, and his imagination had gotten away with him.

In fact, as I walked Shawna to the door, I knew our coven consensus on helping her would be a no. If the hunters turned out to be real, then she could give us a hearty "I told you so." Until then, there was no reason to add to the fear already spreading through town.

Either I was tapping into my intuition, or I was just being stubborn, but I was certain Vincent had been killed by someone in Foxfire Haven, and all the hunter panic was just senseless gossip.

I headed to the kitchen and found Valerian and Marlee at the kitchen table, where they presented very different pictures. Valerian was still in her pajamas and bathrobe, and her long hair was wild and loose. The tip of her tongue was poking out from between her teeth as she focused on measuring a potion into a shot glass.

Marlee, on the other hand, was wearing a red sweater and gray jeans, and her hair was pulled back in its usual neat ponytail. She had a little smile on her face as she went through a stack of sample cocktail napkins.

"I heard you talking to someone. Wyatt again?" Marlee asked without looking up at me.

"No. Shawna, a witch who lives out on the south side of town. She's as worked up over the hunter rumor as anyone else, and she's making pre-packaged protection spells for customers who are also worried. She stopped in to ask if we'd like to do a little freelance work for her, to help prepare and deliver potions."

Valerian stopped pouring and tapped a finger against the shot glass. "Perfect. The Put Your Best Foot Forward potion looks great, and it's going to taste great. Harris will down this in a heartbeat. Wait, what did you say, Hazel?"

I repeated Shawna's request, and Valerian gestured toward her potion when I finished. "I'm doing so well at the tavern that I don't need the extra work. Besides, I don't want another witch learning any of my potion secrets!"

"You tell us everything that goes into them," Marlee pointed out.

"Yes, but you're my coven. That's different."

Marlee and Valerian both agreed with me that saying no was probably our best bet. We'd get Jo's input later, but we expected her to agree with us.

Just as I turned to walk to my bedroom, my coat and scarf slipped off the hooks near the back door and fell to the floor.

"I guess the poltergeist agrees," Valerian quipped. "By the way, I'm trying this potion as soon as Harris shows up at the tavern, and I've got the early shift today. If you ladies want to come out for lunch, maybe you'll get to see the potion in action."

Marlee and I readily agreed to that plan, and I texted Jo to invite her to join us. We all wanted to see Valerian succeed.

Valerian had to get to the tavern by eleven o'clock, but it was nearly one before Marlee and I got there. Jo must have arrived just ahead of us, because she was still settling onto a stool at the bar as Marlee and I walked through the door.

A quick glance showed me that Harris wasn't there, and after I was seated, I caught Valerian's eye. She smiled back. "You haven't missed anything," she assured me.

I was halfway through eating a club sandwich, my favorite thing on the tavern's limited menu, when Harris loudly entered the tavern. He was calling out to Valerian the second he came through the door, telling her he needed her magic touch.

"Ick," Jo said, just loud enough for Marlee's and my ears.

"I've been hearing a lot of rumors about hunters in town," Valerian said smoothly. "And I think you'll agree that we all need to stay positive. I have a new potion called Put Your Best Foot Forward, and it's designed to help all of us project our best selves."

"I'll gladly try that!" Harris was smiling widely, though leering might have been the better term. "I only ever want to put my best self forward when I'm here."

In a flash, Valerian was sliding a pint glass filled with a shimmering green liquid in front of Harris. He lifted the glass and held it high. "Gorgeous color, Val! And that magical sheen is just perfection. Clover?"

"A bit of it, yes," Valerian answered.

"Bottoms up!" Harris raised the glass in Valerian's direction, then brought it to his lips.

It was only then I realized all four of us were staring at Harris in anticipation. We'd been so repulsed by his creepy behavior, but at the moment, we were the creepy ones.

Before Harris could take a drink, his body suddenly lurched forward. Someone had just given him a thump on the back.

"Connor, hey, man!" Harris turned and gave the werewolf a friendly smack on the arm. "I didn't wait for you, obviously. Val's got a new potion on the menu."

Connor reached out and snatched the glass out of Harris's hand. "I ate an awful snack on the way over, and I have to get the taste out of my mouth. I'll buy you another one." In one gulp, Connor drained the glass.

Valerian looked over at us with an expression of utter exasperation, then got to work making another Put Your Best Foot Forward potion.

"Yum!" Connor slammed the empty glass onto the bar. "What does it do, anyway?"

"It's to boost positivity," Harris said. "It even has a bit of clover in it."

"You want some positivity? I'll give it to you! Now that Vincent Draxler is dead, his clients are starting to realize they were just wasting their money with him. I've gotten two of them to sign up with me in the past two days, and a third is planning to sign on for my services tomorrow."

"Good thing you're a shifter and won't mesmerize them like Vincent did." Harris laughed heartily.

"It's a good week to own an advertising business," Connor said.

Connor and Vincent had been business rivals, and Vincent had been using illegal magical tactics to get his clients to spend more money with him than they should. Had he used magic to get those clients, too, and had it negatively affected Connor?

"Territorial dispute," I whispered.

"It wasn't about werewolves versus vampires," Jo said, leaning close to my ear. "It was about advertising clients. Both of them work in marketing and advertising."

Marlee slid off her stool and stood so she was between Jo and me, keeping our circle tight so we could talk quietly. "Connor is elated that Vincent is out of the way."

Jo broke into a grin. "I did this! I wrote an intention that information valuable to the case would be revealed, and Connor just made it come true!"

"You manifested that!" I said, trying to keep my voice quiet.

"With help from Val's potion," Jo clarified. "Now, we just need to know if Connor killed Vincent."

Harris's voice broke into our conversation. "What are you ladies conspiring about down there at that end of the bar?"

"We're celebrating our magical wins," Marlee told him.

"Not as good as the win I got this week," Connor said. "For my next trick, I'm going to kill a hunter."

Chapter Eighteen

I gasped loudly, and Connor laughed. "That's right," he said, his chest bowing out. "I'm not going to let them get away with hunting down shifters."

"We don't even know for certain there are hunters in the area." Valerian rolled her eyes as she walked over to Harris and plunked a fresh potion down in front of him. "It's just a rumor."

"My son saw one," Connor insisted. "Too many people around town have spotted these men for anyone to still believe it's just a rumor. There are hunters here, and we're in danger. I'm sure it's nice for you witches, since you don't have to worry about them coming after you."

Jo began to talk, but she only got out a syllable before Marlee silenced her with a sharp glance. "Let him feel his anger," Marlee murmured. She was picking up on Connor's wrath, and she knew it was fruitless for any of us to try to calm him down.

It was Harris who finally talked some sense into him. "There's nothing you can do right now about the hunters, so you might as well sit down and have a drink."

Connor glared at Jo, Marlee, and me before he settled onto a stool next to Harris. The two of them began speaking in voices too low for us to hear, and we returned to our own conversation, but the feeling of tension hung in the air.

Not surprisingly, Valerian stood behind the bar close to us, putting as much distance as she could between herself and Harris. When he continued to talk quietly with Connor, she whispered to us, "I guess my potion is working. He's not paying any attention to me."

"Good!" Marlee answered, while Jo and I nodded in agreement.

We were wrapping up our lunch, which had continued to go peacefully, when Barry joined us. Instead of sitting in his usual spot at the very end of the bar, he sat down next to Jo. "How's it going, ladies?" he asked.

"Oh, the usual," Jo quipped. "We're ruffling feathers."

Barry chuckled, a pleasant rumbling sound. "I thought that was what your familiars did."

Jo barked out a laugh. "They do it literally. It's metaphorical for us."

"By the way, Barry," I said, leaning around Jo so I could see him better. "You remember telling me that as our power as a coven grew, it would help our poltergeist's power grow, too? Turns out, we're all supercharged. There's some kind of energy in that funeral home, and it's giving all of us a full magical battery."

Barry gave me a knowing look, his golden-brown eyes both interested and sympathetic. "Energy? The kind that someone might search frantically for?"

"Exactly. We might be on the same trail Uncle Grant was."

"Be careful." Barry's eyes moved to Jo. "Please."

"We always are," she assured him. "We're going to figure out what's going on, and how to get it under control."

Valerian swept up just then with Barry's usual drink, an expensive single-malt whiskey, and he raised it in a little toast. "To getting the answers that Grant couldn't."

Barry and my uncle had been friends, and he had once admitted regretting not doing more to help when Grant became obsessed with the alleged hidden treasure at the funeral home. I knew that if we needed Barry's help dealing with this mysterious energy source, which many in the magical world *would* consider a treasure, all we had to do was ask.

"Hey, Bigfoot," Connor called from his end of the bar.

"His name is Barry," Marlee said.

"Right. Barry. Listen, you're in danger, too, as long as these hunters are around."

Something between a hum and a growl came from Barry's throat. I got the impression he wasn't convinced the rumors were true, either.

Connor didn't seem to notice, or perhaps, he didn't care, because he plowed ahead. "I'm getting together a search party for tomorrow night. We'll meet at the Cryptid Caverns Campground at six o'clock in the evening, then fan out and search the woods around there as soon as it's full dark. They can't hide if enough of us are out there looking for them."

"That's not far from my home," Barry commented. "I walk through those woods every day, and I haven't seen anyone."

"Because they're good at hiding, which is why we're going to flush them out and deal with them!"

"Yeah!" Harris pumped a fist.

"If you don't care about your own safety," Connor challenged, "then do it for your community. Foxfire Haven needs you, Bigf—Barry."

"I'll consider it." Barry returned his attention to his whiskey, and Connor's attempts to get more of an answer out of him were thoroughly ignored.

Connor and Harris paid and left twenty minutes later, both looking expectantly at Barry as they left. Harris barely said a word to Valerian.

"Congratulations on a successful potion, Val," Marlee said as soon as the two of them had disappeared out the door.

"Harris didn't tip me nearly as well as he usually does, but not getting a creepy invitation to his cabin is far more valuable than cash."

"It was a shame Connor snatched the first potion out of Harris's hands," Jo said. "But Connor drank that Put Your Best Foot Forward potion, and he sure steered toward positivity. At least, what he considers positive."

"He sure seems happy about the fact that Vincent is dead and, therefore, no longer his rival," I agreed. "That was a very valuable piece of information, and it explains that territorial dispute they got into here at the tavern."

Valerian refilled Barry's glass as she added, "Vincent said Connor was spreading malicious rumors about him. Now, we know it's because Connor had learned his business rival was using magic to trick his clients. If I was in that situation, I'd probably be spreading the word about his unethical approach, too."

Marlee and I left soon after. I had remembered to tell Jo about Shawna's proposal almost as an afterthought, but she quickly agreed with the rest of us that it was a bad idea to get involved. When I glanced back at the bar on my way out the door, I saw Jo scoot a little closer to Barry.

Since Marlee was driving, I used the short time in the car to text Wyatt. I briefly described the business rivalry between Connor and Vincent. It was likely the constables had already dug up that bit of information, but it felt like something worth passing on.

Marlee dropped me off at the end of the driveway so I could check the mail, and I was surprised to find a bright-yellow flyer inside the mailbox. It was a basic design with big bold lettering that proclaimed, *Neighborhood Meeting Tonight!* There was an address for a house one street over, plus a starting time of seven o'clock. Beneath that was a bulleted list of the meeting's agenda. The first read, *Share the latest news about the hunter invasion.*

The fear was spreading, even though, so far, there was no proof we even had something to be afraid of.

I had a delivery to make that afternoon for the tavern, and I enjoyed the quiet drive to and from Stanton. I didn't even tune the radio to a local classic rock station, like I normally did. The silence was exactly what I needed.

When I got back to Foxfire Haven with a hearse full of beer kegs, I parked in the alley behind the tavern. With the help of the tavern's owner, Will, everything was shuttled inside in just a few minutes.

As I was swinging the rear door of the hearse closed, I heard several people talking nearby, and their voices were getting louder. The alley was usually deserted, except for store owners along its length running trash or recycling out to the bins, so I was surprised to have company.

Two burly men were walking down the alley, followed by none other than Shawna. As I watched, one of the men darted to one side to peer behind a pile of empty crates, then returned to his companions.

There was no way Shawna would overlook the hearse, so I prepared to give her our refusal to do freelance work for her business. I waved at her, and before she approached, the two men stepped close and gazed at me intently.

"Um, hello?" I said, taking a step back. One of the men inhaled loudly through his nose, and I got the impression he was sniffing me.

"It's just Hazel," Shawna admonished. To me, she said, "Sorry. We're patrolling, and these two have their hackles up. Figuratively, at any rate, since the moon isn't full."

They were shifters of some kind then. Werewolves, probably.

That guy really was sniffing me.

"On the hunt for hunters?" I asked.

Shawna shrugged. "We expect they're hiding miles from here, but we thought we'd make a sweep of the downtown area, just in case. Connor Ulmann is organizing a search party for tomorrow night, out in the woods. You and your coven should join."

"Are you close with Connor?" I asked.

"Of course. He's the one who designs all the ads for my shop on Alchemy. I do a lot of sales there."

Alchemy was a place to buy and sell magical secondhand items. Apparently, new things could be bought there, too, like Shawna's spell kits. What was more interesting to me was learning that she was a client of Connor's.

Connor was already on my list of suspects for Vincent's murder. Now, I knew that he had a professional relationship with Shawna Sullivan, who was doing a brisk business because of the panic about the hunters.

Had Connor killed Vincent as revenge for his underhanded business ethics? Or had he killed Vincent to help a client get more orders? Shawna was complaining about all the extra help she needed, but maybe, that had been the goal from the very start.

There was another angle I had to consider, too. It was possible I was face-to-face with the killer at that moment, and I had two on-edge werewolves breathing down my neck. Had Shawna herself killed Vincent to fuel the rumors and boost her business?

Chapter Nineteen

SHAWNA TOOK A STEP toward me. "Hazel?"

I blinked. How long had I been staring at her while all those thoughts raced through my mind? "What?"

"I mentioned Alchemy, and it was like you froze."

I shook my head, more to clear it than to counter Shawna's comment. "I only recently learned about that site. Living in the non-magical world for more than twenty years means I missed out on some things."

"We might have magic, but we need our technology, too." Shawna gestured to the two men. "Come on, let's head on back. We need to finish up those Seek and Find charm kits before tomorrow's search party."

Shawna began to turn away from me, but she stopped and asked, "What did your coven say about working for me?"

I cleared my throat and looked down at the dirty asphalt. "Oh, um, we're going to have to decline. It's just, Jo is always working late at the newspaper, and Val has been busier than ever because her potions are so popular, and—"

Shawna clapped me on the shoulder, startling me into silence. "I get it! I always say being a witch is busy business! But if you change your minds, you know how to find me."

I felt myself relax as Shawna and the men walked past me and continued down the alley. I wasn't sure why I had felt so nervous about turning down her offer, though I expected her Type A personality had something to do with it. She was one intense witch.

Plus, there was that whole "she might have killed Vincent" thing.

When I got home, I hollered a hello to Marlee before disappearing into the bathroom for a long soak in the bathtub. My brain felt like it was aching, but since there was nothing I could do about that, I settled for soothing my muscles, instead.

I was so worn out that I dozed off, and I only woke up when the water had gone cold. I hastily got out of the tub, dried off, and snuggled into flannel pajamas and fuzzy slippers.

When I walked into the kitchen to see about making dinner, I spotted Marlee hunched over her planner at the table. She looked up and began to laugh.

"Hazel, you know it's only five o'clock, right?"

I looked down at myself. "I didn't know, but that's okay. I'm not going anywhere tonight."

"Not even to the neighborhood meeting?" Marlee waved her pen in the air. "I can't imagine anything more fun than being in someone's living room, surrounded by a couple dozen panicked neighbors."

"You are definitely not attending," I told her. "The way your magic has been escalating, the neighbor hosting the meeting might find a hurricane in their kitchen."

"Jo is going. She claims she's covering it for the newspaper, but I think she's simply curious to see what happens."

"Good. She can give us a full report later."

"I can give you a report right now." Holman had materialized next to the table, and he was staring down at me with a look of supreme disappointment. "I'm here to report that it isn't even fully dark outside, and you're in pajamas. And not just pajamas, but that awful, oversized plaid ensemble that makes you look very unattractive."

"I'm not trying to look attractive," I retorted. "I want to be warm and comfy, and I am, so there!" It was a childish response, but at least I resisted the urge to stick my tongue out at him.

Holman heaved a sigh. "Marlee is still dressed nicely."

"Thank you, Holman." She smiled sweetly at him.

A sudden idea struck me. "Holman, I want you to do something for me. You're upset that I'm in my pajamas so early, right?" I reached down and grabbed one of my fuzzy slippers, then placed it on the table. "Go ahead and take out your frustration on my slipper. Just knock it right off the table."

"You know I can't manipulate physical objects."

"Humor me."

"I humor you and your wardrobe every single day of my existence." Holman lifted his eyes to the ceiling. "I'll make a deal with you. I'll do this as a favor to you, but in turn, you have to go put on real clothes."

"Fine," I grumbled.

Holman stared at the slipper for a long moment. His face always had an expression of disdain on it, but as he continued to stare, it shifted into a look of concentration. Suddenly, his right arm shot out, and he slapped the slipper.

It didn't fall off the table, but it did scoot a few inches across the surface. Marlee gasped while I shouted, "I knew it!"

Holman stared at his upturned palm, his mouth open. "I had no idea I was so powerful."

"You weren't," I told him, "but you are now. The poltergeist isn't the only ghost benefitting from the extra energy around here. You hit the table the other day, and I thought I felt it move. Now, I know I didn't imagine it."

A mischievous smile spread across Holman's face. With his pencil mustache and old-fashioned suit, he looked like the villain in a nineteen thirties gangster movie. "What else can I do?" he asked, then disappeared.

Marlee giggled nervously. "Telling Holman he can move physical objects has the potential to backfire spectacularly."

"Unfortunately, I did not think about that before testing his ability." I put my slipper on my foot again and leaned back in the chair.

"You have to change before you can relax," Marlee reminded me, tapping the end of her pen on the table for emphasis. "You promised Holman."

"There's going to be no living with him now." I got up and went into my bedroom, where I begrudgingly changed into a royal-blue sweater and black jeans. I was still comfortable, but Holman wouldn't be able to say I hadn't held up my end of the deal.

Luckily, my encounter with Holman was the most exciting part of my night. Jo got home around eight o'clock, and she filled us in on the neighborhood meeting. It had gone exactly as I had expected it to, with lots of hand-wringing and promises to catch the hunters before they caught one of our town's vampires or werewolves.

Jo had also said that most neighbors agreed Vincent's death had been at the hands of a hunter, so that rumor was still going strong.

I woke up Monday morning with a feeling of anxious anticipation. Maybe it was the report Jo had brought us from the neighborhood meeting, or the fact that the search party Connor was organizing was that night.

My heightened state could also have been the result of the dream I'd had, in which a pack of werewolves had sniffed me until I promised to put on their favorite perfume.

While the four of us chatted over our coffee that morning, Valerian suggested we participate in the search party.

"You're kidding, right?" I asked. "The search party isn't going to find anyone, because there are no hunters in town."

Jo held up a finger. "There could be, though I agree with you that it's unlikely."

"Besides," Valerian continued, "I'm not suggesting we go to find hunters. I think we should go to find clues."

"I don't follow." I looked down at my mostly empty cup. Maybe I needed more coffee to understand what Valerian had in mind.

Marlee's eyes lit up, so she, at least, got the gist of what Valerian was saying. "It's a chance to observe everyone participating! We can chat with our fellow volunteers in the hope of learning something."

"That's right." Valerian nodded. "And we'll bring our familiars, because they'll be a welcome addition to the search, thanks to their keen senses."

We all agreed to join the search party, and I mentally penciled in a nap for that afternoon. It was probably going to be a long, cold night.

The rest of my day was rather humdrum in the best kind of way. I enjoyed making several deliveries, running into someone I knew when I stopped at the supermarket, and taking a well-deserved nap in the early afternoon.

Before long, though, it was time to bundle up and head to the campground on the edge of town. Foxfire Haven was surrounded by forested land, but if Connor was intent on searching the wilderness, he had to start somewhere. The campground, at least, had a sizable dirt parking lot where the volunteers could gather.

Marlee drove the four of us, and our familiars, in her compact SUV. It would have been fine, except Gordon took up a shocking amount of space, and every time Marlee hit a bump, he would squawk in protest.

Finally, though, we were at the campground. At least fifty other people were already there, huddled around a small wooden platform set up at one end of the parking lot. We joined the throng, and I heard several people exclaim happily at the sight of our familiars.

I walked up next to Gnorris, the owner of the Growing Power Garden Store. He had one hand wrapped around the end of his long white beard, and he looked like he was slowly tugging on it.

"You okay, Gnorris?" I asked.

Gnorris looked up at me, his face only slightly higher than my knee. "I'm not a big fan of crowds like this. Makes me feel a bit claustrophobic."

"We can make space for you," I said, nodding toward the rest of my coven.

"Yes, please."

Gordon, who stood nearly as tall as Gnorris, swooped down next to the gnome while the rest of us formed a wide circle around them both. I saw Gnorris's body relax as he stroked Gordon's broad back. With us around him, Gnorris didn't have to worry about being crushed by people more than twice his height.

As the last of the light faded from the sky, Connor climbed onto the wooden platform and announced we'd be starting in twenty minutes, so any participating vampires had time to drive to the campground. I passed the time by chatting with Gnorris and my coven.

Just as Connor was getting up to address us all again, I felt a tap on my shoulder and turned to see Adeline standing there, looking even more uncomfortable than Gnorris had.

Adeline addressed me, even though her eyes were on the fir trees above our heads. "Good evening, Hazel."

"Adeline! I'm surprised to see you here. After everything you've been through with Vincent's murder, I figured you'd want to stay away from anything having to do with it."

Even as I said that, I spotted a few people around us giving Adeline sidelong glances.

"Call it a PR move on my part," Adeline said quietly. "Even people who believe this hunter rumor seem to think I might have had a hand in Vincent's death."

"You don't believe the rumor, either?"

Adeline shook her head, and her voice was even quieter as she answered, "If it were true, they would have come after me by now. But if there are no hunters, then suspicion falls back on me, doesn't it? Being out here and pretending we're going to catch some bad guys is the best thing I can do for my reputation right now."

Before I could answer, Connor began addressing the crowd. He thanked everyone for attending, then laid out his plan. There were three trails leading away from the campground, and we'd split into groups to cover all of them while a few people remained in the parking lot to help as needed. Once on the trails, we could fan out into the trees on either side to cover a wider swath of land.

The four of us in the coven split up, figuring we might learn more if we were in different groups. With Perkins perched on my shoulder, I joined a group that was taking a trail heading south. Just as our group began to walk down the sharp slope at the trailhead, I heard my name being called.

It was Wyatt, and I was even more surprised to see him than I had been to see Adeline.

"Hazel, why don't you hang back and walk with me?" he asked. Even in the darkness, with just flashlights and starlight to illuminate the trail, I could see how nervous he looked. "There's something I need to tell you."

CHAPTER TWENTY

WYATT SLOWED HIS PACE, and I matched it as the rest of our search group moved ahead. I had my flashlight pointed at the trail directly in front of me, and I kept my eyes on it as we walked in silence. I wasn't sure if Wyatt was waiting for the nearest people to be out of earshot, or if he was simply mustering up the courage to say whatever it was he wanted to say.

Finally, after a few minutes, the rest of our group disappeared around a long left-hand bend in the trail. Perkins hooted softly, and I glanced down to see him scrunched down on my shoulder, his head swiveling from one side of the trail to the other.

I could relate to his feeling of unease. The fir trees towering overhead felt cold and oppressive, and I instinctively took a step closer to Wyatt. Our shoulders brushed, and I immediately stepped away again. Then, I silently said the incantation for shedding my magic. The excess I'd built up seemed terribly bright as it puffed from my body, but when I glanced over my shoulder, it had created a soft, glowing trail. I told myself that, at any rate, we wouldn't get lost.

If Wyatt had noticed my exhalation, he didn't comment on it. He continued on in silence, occasionally sweeping his bright flashlight into the woods on either side. Finally, he said quietly, "I wasn't entirely honest with you and your coven."

"Honest about what?" I kept my tone gentle.

Wyatt ran his free hand through his hair, looked back, then stopped walking. It was so unexpected that I continued on a couple paces before I realized what had happened.

"I told you necromancy is a complicated magic, and that I hadn't been able to use it on the murder victims who have turned up since you came back to Foxfire Haven."

"Yes, I remember."

"It is a complicated magic, but that's not the reason I haven't used it recently."

"What's the reason, then?"

"I lost my magic." Wyatt licked his lips, his flashlight darting from side to side.

He's going to make me drag this out of him, one detail at a time, I thought. "How did you lose your magic?"

Even before Wyatt spoke, I realized I knew the answer. "Oh," I said sadly. "Constance."

Wyatt's eyes shot to my face. "How did you know?"

"Whenever you've talked about her, it's obvious you still feel grief about losing her." Wyatt had told me his wife had died of cancer, and even though it had happened years before I returned to my hometown, I could tell the loss still hurt. "That affected your magic, didn't it?"

"Yeah," Wyatt said shortly. "It's like she died, and a part of me died, too. I even tried to talk to her after she'd passed, but I couldn't get so much as a single word from her."

The mental image of Wyatt desperately trying to have one last conversation with his deceased wife was heartbreaking, and I was at a loss for words. If it had been anyone else, I would have pulled them into a tight hug and said nothing.

At the rate I'd been going with Wyatt, though, one hug would turn into a magical exhalation so strong I might uproot the surrounding trees.

"How many people know?" I asked once the silence became too uncomfortable. "About you losing your necromancy, I mean?"

"The other constables, of course. A few friends." Wyatt paused. "Now, you, and the rest of your coven, once you tell them."

"Do you want me to tell them?"

"I would appreciate it. Saves me from having to say it all over again."

I wasn't ready to hug Wyatt, but I did reach out and put a sympathetic hand on his arm. Unfortunately, when I did, I felt a jolt like I had earlier with him. "Just like the ATM," I mumbled.

"You mean the one that was broken last week? Did you do that?"

"It wasn't accepting my PIN, but I knew I had the right numbers, and I got really frustrated, and I just—" I reached out a finger and made a stabbing motion.

Wyatt chuckled. "And, now, you're trying to zap me, too? Be careful. You can't just hang an *Out of Order* sign on me, you know."

The moment helped us move on from our discussion about Wyatt's lost magic, and after that, we were able to carry on a fairly normal conversation. Except, instead of talking about the woods we were in or how nicely the weather had cooperated for the search, we talked about hunters. Wyatt said his phone had been ringing all day with people claiming to have spotted a hunter, and if every report was to be believed, there were more than forty hunters in the area.

Slowly, we caught up to our search group. Some people had fanned out and were searching the underbrush on either side of the trail, but everyone looked slightly bored.

After an hour of walking, we reached the end of the trail, where it merged with the other two and became one wide path. One of the other search groups was already there, and I caught sight of Marlee talking to Adeline. Stella was flying low circles over the group, her orange beak almost seeming to glow in the darkness.

People in each group began to chat, and a couple of burly men I didn't know approached Wyatt. "We've found nothing," one of them said.

"Except a few deer," added the other.

"Same here," Wyatt told them. He pointed at each man, then at me, as he said, "Tank and Shotgun, Hazel Underwood."

"Oh, the hearse lady!" the one called Shotgun enthused. He raised an arm and flexed his bicep. "If you ever have something heavy to deliver, Tank and I are always on call."

I smiled. "I appreciate it. You two are brothers?"

"Brothers, and werewolves," Tank said. "We don't buy into this hunter nonsense, but a lot of shifters are feeling scared, so we're doing what we can to help."

I glanced at Wyatt. "We're not convinced, either, but if our search party can help alleviate some fears, then that's a good thing."

There was a babble of voices from somewhere on the far side of our group, and all four of us looked sharply in that direction. Wyatt's body tensed, like he was ready to spring into action, and the brothers lifted their heads and sniffed the air.

Seriously, why did werewolves sniff so much?

Tank, who was the tallest of our group, relaxed. "Aw, it's just the third group."

"What do we do now?" I asked. We would already have an hour-long walk back to the parking lot, but I didn't know if we were supposed to keep going now that our trail had hit its end. It wasn't late by any means, but it was dark and chilly. I reached up and gave Perkins a pat on the head, and he scooted closer to my neck so he could bury his face in the collar of my coat.

"Tank and I are going to keep going down this main path, until we reach the caverns ahead," Shotgun said. "For everyone else, Connor said he wanted the groups to swap trails when they turn back. We'll go back on the trail that brought you here."

"You let me know if the two of you find anything farther down the trail," Wyatt told the brothers.

"Yes, Chief Constable. And you two enjoy your evening." Tank glanced at me and quirked his eyebrow ever so slightly. He clearly thought Wyatt and I were out on more than a search-party stroll.

Once the two brothers had moved off, I heard a screech. It didn't sound human, and my first thought was that Perkins had put his beak right next to my ear and yelled at me. When the screech sounded again, I looked over and saw Stella dive-bombing a group of people. I couldn't see Marlee anymore, and I instantly hurried in Stella's direction.

"Wait!" Wyatt snapped. He jumped forward and grabbed my hand. "We don't know what's going on."

"If Stella is upset, something is wrong with Marlee," I said. I started moving again, and although Wyatt didn't drop my hand, he did let me propel him forward.

I heard a few raised voices, including a man who shouted, "Stupid bird! That hurt!"

I also heard a woman cry, "Help her sit down!"

Marlee was leaning heavily on a young man's arm, her head drooping. Soft raindrops were falling onto her and the man.

"Get her away from the crowd," I instructed calmly. "She's overwhelmed with emotion."

The man gave me a puzzled look, but he dutifully helped Marlee to a fallen tree a short distance away from the three search groups. "Thank you," she whispered as she sat down on the thick, moss-covered trunk.

"Thanks. We've got it from here," Wyatt told the man.

"Marlee, what happened?" I asked as I sat down next to her. I put an arm around her, and she sagged against my shoulder.

"I'm not the one who needs help." Marlee's hand twitched, and she pointed slowly toward the crowd. "It's Val. Harris won't leave her alone."

It was Harris who had been shouting that Stella hurt him. He'd been harassing Valerian, and the toucan stood up for her. I expected Lonnie had joined the fight, too.

"He'll leave her alone when I'm done with him," Wyatt said. He turned and rushed toward Stella, who was circling over the heads of searchers again. As I watched, she dove straight down, her screech echoing in the woods around us.

Chapter Twenty-One

"Everyone is afraid," Marlee whispered. "All the strong emotions were getting to be too much already, but suddenly, Val's anger flared, and it just about knocked me off my feet."

"Why was she angry?" I was watching Wyatt as I listened, and I silently wished him luck.

"Her group just came out of the woods into this clearing, and I could feel her before I could see her. I found her, and Harris was glued to her side. Val told him to leave her alone, and I guess Stella took that as a sign to shoo him away. Lonnie helped, too."

Despite the seriousness of the situation, I smiled at the thought of Stella and Lonnie standing up for Valerian.

Marlee breathed in deeply. "You feel surprisingly calm, Haze."

"Do I?" I looked down at myself, as if I might see some outward sign of my apparent zen state. Marlee was right, though: even though I was concerned for Valerian, I knew she had Stella and Wyatt standing up for her. Marlee would recover from her overwhelm in a short while, so I wasn't worried about her, either. "You knew Wyatt was hiding something when he told us about being a necromancer. He told me the truth just now, and I think maybe it's why I'm feeling calm. I like knowing why he was acting so defensively at dinner."

"It wasn't us and our questions about being a necromancer that bothered him," Marlee guessed.

I told Marlee about Wyatt losing his magic when he'd lost his wife, and when I was done, all she said was, "Oh, that's so sad. Poor Wyatt."

"Yeah. And, after he confessed that to me, I touched his arm, and I wound up zapping him with my magic." I laughed at the absurdity of my exhalations. "He probably thought I was trying to rub in the fact that I have magic, and he doesn't."

"He knows better," Marlee assured me. "When you two came over here with me, I felt his concern for me. But I felt something else, too. It was a sort of peace. A lot like what you're feeling, in fact."

"Wyatt and I just hiked through the woods together, and we didn't get into a single stupid argument, so I think we'll both be celebrating that."

Wyatt had disappeared into the crowd, but I heard some shouting from the direction he'd gone, and then Stella zoomed up to a branch, where she perched proudly. A few seconds later, Tank and Shotgun emerged from the crowd. Harris was between them, and each brother had one of his arms. They were escorting him down a trail, in the direction of the parking lot.

I couldn't see Harris's face clearly, but Marlee could feel him even at that distance. "Ooh, he's hopping mad."

"Val should have packed that Put Your Best Foot Forward potion for the search tonight."

Marlee sat up straight and nudged me with her elbow. "Go ahead, I know you want to check on Val."

"I'll be right back," I promised her.

Finding Valerian was easy because Stella's perch was directly above where she and Wyatt were standing. Wyatt and Valerian were talking earnestly, and Valerian's hands were flying as she gestured wildly. Marlee had been right about Valerian being absolutely fed up with Harris. I knew that the more aggravated she got, the more dramatic her gestures became. Lonnie seemed to be punctuating Valerian's story, cawing now and then for emphasis.

I stood to one side while Wyatt and Valerian finished their conversation. A lot of people around us were also watching them, but as the minutes ticked by, they gradually lost interest.

Connor raised his voice and began to issue instructions for the return search. Several people volunteered to continue on until they reached the caverns at the end of the trail, and I noticed that Tank and Shotgun were among them. Harris had been successfully kicked out of the party.

Two of the search groups moved off, beginning the trek back to the parking lot, while those who were going on began walking toward the caverns.

That left the third group huddled together with Connor at their center. I couldn't see him, but I could hear his deep voice as he addressed the group.

There was a flash of a plaid flannel jacket next to me, topped by a pair of pigtails. It was Shawna, and she had about ten long black necklaces around her neck. Each one had a wire-wrapped crystal dangling from the end, as well as a small silk sachet that gave off a strong odor of garlic.

I pressed a finger against my nostrils to block the smell. “Hi, Shawna,” I said, my voice slightly nasal.

“It stinks, I know.” Shawna didn’t sound at all embarrassed by the cloud of scent enveloping her. “But these are my Seek and Find charms. Portable and affordable! I had about thirty at the beginning of the evening, but they’re selling fast.”

“Has your search group found anything yet?”

“No. But I see we had a stalker in our midst. You know, I have a pre-packaged spell kit to get rid of unwanted visitors. You could easily modify it for unwanted barflies, too. Harris has always been a weird one, so I would suggest Valerian do the spell as soon as possible. Has he invited her to his cabin yet?”

I nodded. “I understand he uses that pick-up line on a lot of women.”

“A lot of witches,” Shawna corrected. “I think he’s more interested in having someone whose magic he can use than having a love connection. He’s a witch, too, but he’s always been good at linking up with witches who have stronger magic than he does.”

That made sense, since Harris hadn’t been interested in Valerian until she’d started producing one popular potion after another.

Wyatt and Valerian had finished their talk, and they both turned in my direction. Valerian looked a lot calmer, but Wyatt was clearly tired and frustrated. He was already dealing with a vampire slayer on the loose and a town on the verge of mass panic, so I figured adding Harris to the mix was one thing too many.

"I can help," Shawna said to Wyatt.

Wyatt tilted his head slightly. "With what?"

Shawna waved her hands in front of Wyatt, her fingers flexing. "This vibe. Your aura is electric right now. You need my ready-made calming potion. I have clients who say it's the only thing that can get them to sleep at night. I'll even give you a discount since you're a constable."

Valerian looked like she wanted to comment, and I wondered if she was thinking of her own calming potion, which she had given to Wyatt out of kindness rather than for money. Instead, she just lifted her head and gazed at Stella and Lonnie. "Good girls," she called.

Stella squawked proudly in answer, and Lonnie stretched out her long wings.

"Thanks, Shawna, but I think I'll sleep just fine," Wyatt said.

"Suit yourself. But don't think you can just waltz into the magic store and find ingredients that will be as effective. Adeline doesn't have half the ingredients I use. They're all special order, and you can only get them from me."

"I don't carry half the stuff you do, because you use things more typically found in dark magic." Adeline had come up behind us, and I jumped at the sound of her voice. I knew vampires could be quiet, but I'd never had one sneak up on me before, so until that moment, I'd never fully appreciated how stealthy they could be.

"Spoken like someone who's jealous," Shawna said. She had struck me as an aggressive woman but not a malicious one. I was more worried about her trying to sell me magical items I didn't need than her being mean to me. But her demeanor changed entirely as she turned to stand face-to-face with Adeline.

I shot Wyatt a look, and he gave the slightest nod. I had already considered that Shawna might have killed Vincent to get herself more business, and now, I was even more inclined to find it likely. By framing Adeline, her competitor for selling magical items, Shawna would get even more customers.

"I don't mind a bit of friendly competition," Adeline said. Her voice was loud, carrying just like it had the day I'd heard her lecturing Vincent at Into the Cauldron. People began to turn in our direction, and I knew it was not the impression she wanted to make. "What I take offense to is anyone who helps vampires do spells for psychic influence."

"What my clients do with my products is their business," Shawna said.

"You knew exactly what Vincent was doing. He told me himself that he sometimes went to you for help manipulating his advertising clients."

Connor pushed his way past a few onlookers and stepped up to Shawna. "What?" he roared.

"Don't listen to her," Shawna said curtly.

"You told me you didn't work with Vincent." Connor's voice dropped, the anger giving way to hurt. "You told me you were trying to help me get him out of the way."

"And I was."

"But you were helping him at the same time."

Shawna's mouth tightened, but she squared her shoulders and looked Connor in the eyes. "I have bills to pay. I can't be picky about who I sell my products to."

Adeline had a look of glee on her face. She was thoroughly enjoying the confrontation.

Connor, however, looked crushed. His face fell, and it looked like his chin stretched forward. His skull began to shift, taking on a longer, sleeker look.

"He's turning!" Valerian shouted.

Shifters changed into their animal form during the full moon, but if their emotions were heightened enough, they would shift no matter what phase the moon was in. Connor was so angry and hurt he was turning into a werewolf, right there in front of us.

And, if that happened, there was no telling what that would mean for Shawna.

Or, really, for any of us.

CHAPTER TWENTY-TWO

THERE WAS A LOUD ripping sound as Connor's back expanded beyond the confines of his jacket. His spine arched and lengthened as his head continued to elongate. Long, dark fur sprouted from his face and neck.

Wyatt stepped in front of me, his arms held out to the sides. "Back away, slowly," he told me, quietly but firmly.

I tried, really, but my feet were frozen in place. I was so terrified that all I could do was look at the werewolf taking shape.

"All of you," Wyatt insisted. "Back away."

It took a lot of effort to get my feet moving, and my shoes felt like they were full of lead, but I eventually began to shuffle backward. Everyone around us followed suit, leaving just Wyatt to face down Connor.

As I continued to cautiously back up, my shoulder brushed against someone. I flicked my eyes to the side and saw Marlee. She should have been seated on the log, resting and safely out of the way. Instead, she was slowly moving toward Connor.

"Marlee?" I asked in a shaky voice.

"I've got this."

I wasn't sure I believed that. Marlee was unsteady on her legs, and she had her arms held out to help balance herself. She was breathing deeply, too, still exhausted from the empathic overwhelm she'd experienced earlier.

Valerian stepped up to me and took my hand. When I looked at her, I saw that Jo had joined us. She was on the other side of Valerian, and their hands were linked, too.

Jo's eyes were wide, and she whispered, "A few of us veered off to check out a narrow side trail, and we clearly missed some drama. What happened?"

"We'll fill you in soon," Valerian promised. "Ladies, Marlee needs her coven." At that, Valerian bravely began moving forward. Jo and I fell into step with her.

Marlee said something to Wyatt, and although I couldn't hear her words, I saw the way his head shook. Then, I heard her say clearly, "Please."

Wyatt looked from Connor to Marlee, then stepped sideways. He was moving out of the way for Marlee, but he wasn't going to go far.

Jo, Valerian, and I stepped up right behind Marlee, still holding hands. "We'll help" was all Valerian said, and Marlee nodded once.

"Connor," Marlee said loudly. He had nearly finished transforming, and his glare fixed on Marlee as he dropped to all fours. "You feel betrayed. Is that worth doing harm to another person?"

Connor growled in answer.

I couldn't see Marlee's face since we were standing behind her, but I could see the way her shoulders tensed.

Her head dropped, and she slowly brought her hands up to either side of her head. "I feel it, too, Connor."

A bright flash lit up the clearing, the trees around us standing out like solemn sentinels for a heartbeat, and it was followed closely by a loud clap of thunder. Rain began to fall heavily onto Connor's contorted body.

Connor howled, and the sound was so loud I nearly let go of Valerian's hand so I could cover my ears. He looked up at the sky right as lightning ripped across the heavy clouds.

When the thunder echoed through the woods for a second time, Connor crouched down. I didn't know a werewolf could look bewildered, but he managed to do it.

Slowly, Connor's body began to shift again, and I knew he was reverting to his human form. In a few minutes, a soaking-wet man was kneeling on the ground in front of us. The rain slowed, then stopped, and the clouds dispersed. The werewolf and the storm were both gone.

Connor lifted his eyes to Wyatt. "I'm sorry."

"You're lucky you didn't hurt anyone." Wyatt gestured at Marlee. "You have her to thank for that."

Connor's gaze moved to Marlee, who rocked backward on her heels. Jo, Valerian, and I all reached out to steady her.

"You understood what I was feeling," Connor said slowly. "You made it storm because you knew it would help snap me out of it."

Marlee nodded weakly. "It was the weather equivalent of slapping you across the face. You needed a sudden shock."

I looked around at the crowd, which was slowly closing in around us now that the immediate danger had passed. There was no sign of Shawna, and I assumed she was wisely staying out of Connor's line of sight. Adeline was there, though, looking stunned but also slightly smug.

"Shawna is a client of mine," Connor said, as if that explained everything we'd just witnessed.

"You do her advertising for her, right?" I asked.

Connor nodded. "Mostly for her online business. I'm supposed to get a small flat fee and a percentage of the online sales. She's raking in the money, but I haven't gotten my cut in three months. She keeps claiming she's broke, but that can't be true. Plus, she was giving me spells to use against Vincent, but now I know she was selling him magic, too."

"You getting mad at Shawna wasn't just about her not paying you," Wyatt said, nodding. He was writing in his notebook, recording every detail.

Connor made a low growling noise, and I tensed, expecting him to start turning again. "She knows he's my rival! She's been helping him mesmerize customers, all while telling me she was helping me out. She was playing both of us."

"Was Shawna just helping Vincent work magic on his clients, or was she helping him work magic against you, too?" I hadn't really meant to say that out loud. It was more like a thought that accidentally escaped through my mouth, and I quickly looked around again for Shawna. She was still nowhere to be seen, though, so I didn't know if she had heard me.

"I don't know," Connor said. "I just want to get my money, and I want these hunters to get out of town. Then I can go back to my normal life."

Adeline snorted loudly. "You stopped being normal a long time ago."

Several people in the crowd began to murmur, and Adeline pressed her lips together. Apparently, I wasn't the only one saying things that should have remained as internal monologue.

Connor, though, wasn't going to let it go. "You're the one who has a problem with me being a shifter."

"I never said that!" Adeline moved closer to Connor and gazed up at him defiantly. "I told you that your interest in magic was dangerous, and that you needed to think before you did something you couldn't undo. It wasn't about you being a shifter. It was about you not being a witch but thinking you could wield magic like one, and gray magic, no less. When I refused to help you, you went to Shawna because you knew she didn't care. She would gladly let you ruin your life by using magic you don't understand."

There was a collective gasp from the crowd, and Wyatt issued a warning to Adeline. "Maybe this is a conversation we should have at the station."

"Why not have it right now?" Shawna appeared between a group of women—none other than Natalie and her coven—and strode right up to Adeline. "You've always hated me because my potions and spells are better than yours."

"I sell items and ingredients, not ready-made magic," Adeline retorted. "I think witches should know how to make their own potions and spells, and I think their magic is stronger when someone isn't doing the work for them. But it's not just about that, Shawna. I'm tired of you stealing business from me."

"You said you liked healthy competition."

"Not when my competition is encouraging people to use dark magic. Vincent should have never—"

Adeline didn't get to finish her rant, because Natalie picked that exact moment to step forward. "If you ran a better business, you wouldn't be losing customers!"

Natalie's coven closed in behind her, forming a semi-circle. It was almost a mirror image of the way my coven was standing, except we'd done it to help Marlee de-escalate a werewolf situation. They were doing it to help Natalie bully Adeline.

"This is not the time to be bringing up that nonsense," Adeline warned. Instead of yelling, she spoke in a low, even tone. It was more terrifying than any shouting could have been.

Natalie, Adeline, and Shawna were all glaring at each other. Behind them, Connor was twitching slightly, as if he were fighting the urge to begin shifting into his werewolf form again. Wyatt was carefully watching the scene, not intervening yet but ready to jump in if needed.

I thought of Vincent, and the way he was connected to the people standing there. Adeline had been against Vincent's use of manipulative magic, which he'd wanted to use to help mesmerize helpless advertising clients. Since Adeline wouldn't budge, Vincent had gone to Shawna for help. Shawna, who seemed to have few ethical guidelines for her witchy business, had happily been supplying Vincent with magical solutions.

Add in the fact that Connor had been doing advertising work for Shawna—who still owed him money—and using magic against Vincent, and things were even more complicated.

What a tangled web, I thought.

It was a lot of drama, and Natalie's coven seemed to be enjoying every second of it. Two of the women had small smiles on their lips, and the other looked like she was ready to pounce on Adeline.

Meanwhile, Marlee was still leaning back against Jo, Valerian, and me. I glanced over at Valerian and Jo. "I'm glad we're not scandalous witches," I said quietly.

"It's a lot more fun to write newspaper articles about them than to be one," Jo agreed. I knew she would ordinarily have her notebook out so she could jot down details for the article she was probably already penning in her mind. But, with one hand on Marlee's back, Jo had to settle for observing and trying to remember everything that was happening.

Perkins was still on my shoulder, and I looked around to see where the rest of our familiars were. Stella had remained on the branch above Connor's head, and I wondered if she had gotten soaked in Marlee's rainstorm. Lonnie had settled next to her, and Gordon was on a thicker branch just below the two of them.

My gaze traveled from the familiars back down to the standoff between the two witches and the vampire, and as it did, I heard a sudden humming noise. The sound started somewhere behind me, and I caught a blur of motion that whizzed right past Valerian's head.

As I instinctively pulled Valerian toward me, I caught the sound of something striking the tree where Stella,

Lonnie, and Gordon were perched. Wyatt trained his flashlight on the trunk of the tree, and a few people nearby cried out in fear.

Someone had shot an arrow into the crowd, and it had embedded itself in the tree trunk.

Chapter Twenty-Three

THE ENTIRE CROWD FELL silent for the span of a few seconds. I think we were all standing there, holding our breath, wondering if another arrow was going to come sailing out of the woods.

Then, suddenly, everything erupted into utter chaos.

Enough people began screaming that I couldn't hear what Valerian was saying, even though she was right next to me. A few people fell down onto the ground and covered their heads, but most began to run. The ones who still had a bit of sense headed back down the trails we had taken, so they would wind up at the parking lot eventually. Unfortunately, in the panic, some people headed away from the parking lot, and I wondered how long it would be before they realized their error.

Wyatt ran, too, except he went in the direction the arrow had come from.

Natalie's coven pushed past us, nearly knocking Marlee to the ground. "What are you waiting for?" Natalie admonished as she went.

"Get Marlee back to the log," I yelled to Valerian and Jo. Slowly, trying to move so we wouldn't get tackled by someone in a panic, we made our way back to the log Marlee had been sitting on earlier.

We got there just in time. Marlee sank down onto it and folded the top half of her body until her forehead was on her knees. "At least the emotions are heading away from us," she said quietly.

"We'll wait here until the searchers have had a chance to clear out," Jo assured her. "We don't want to get you back to the parking lot, only to find another group of scared people."

"I'm not sure we should be here," Valerian said, gazing around. "We're sitting ducks for whomever shot that arrow."

"I doubt they were aiming for us, though that arrow did get awfully close to you, Val," I said as I rubbed Marlee's back, trying to send her all the calm energy I could. Because, despite the situation, I wasn't afraid at the moment. The people who had panicked had worried me more than the arrow itself had.

Actually, I was a little afraid. I didn't want Wyatt to get himself into trouble. At the same time, though, I knew he was tough enough to face down the rogue archer.

"Who were they aiming for, do you think?" Valerian asked. "And do you think it's the same person who murdered Vincent?"

I shrugged. "I don't know the answer to either. However, a bow and arrow seems like an awfully old-fashioned way of killing someone."

"It's a favorite among hunters," Jo pointed out. "Supernatural hunters, I mean."

"And I expect we were all meant to think that shot came from a hunter." I gestured toward the clearing, where only a few people still remained. "Someone wanted to cause a panic."

"But why?" Marlee asked, her voice muffled against her jeans. "Did Adeline hire someone to pose as a hunter, so she would no longer seem like a suspect in Vincent's death?"

"Maybe it really was a hunter," Valerian said doubtfully.

"A hunter wouldn't have missed." Jo sat down on the log and whistled. Gordon swooped down out of the tree and landed in front of her. "Gordie, I need a favor. That arrow is evidence, and we don't want anyone touching it. Can you and the other familiars guard it?"

Gordon squawked loudly, opened his massive beak, then shut it with a snap.

"Ouch," Valerian said. "Is that what he'll do to anyone who tries to touch the arrow?"

"If it comes to it." Jo smiled proudly at her pelican as he flew back to the tree, roused Stella and Lonnie, then took up a position on the ground directly underneath the arrow. Stella and Lonnie settled on each side of him while Perkins flew from my shoulder to land on Gordon's back. His head swiveled around, getting a much wider view than the other birds could.

Marlee lifted her head and giggled weakly at the sight.

"We'll stay here until you feel better," Jo told her.

"And until Wyatt comes back," I added.

Wyatt returned long before Marlee felt recovered enough to make the long walk back to the parking lot. We heard the crunching of twigs and leaves, then he appeared not far from where we sat. "What are you four still doing here?"

"Marlee needs more time to recover," I said, "and our familiars are guarding the arrow for you."

"Oh." Wyatt's look of concerned annoyance softened. "Thank you. I've got constables on the way, so they can help try to track down our mystery archer."

"This just turned into a real search party." Jo pointed at the arrow. "And I don't think you're looking for a hunter, because they wouldn't have missed."

"Unless they were aiming for the tree." Wyatt loped over to the log and sat down next to me. He winced and pressed a hand to his lower back. "I'm getting too old for chasing people through the woods."

"No sign of the archer, I suppose?" I asked.

Wyatt gazed toward the line of trees nearest us. "I expect they ran the second after shooting that arrow into the crowd. They had easy access to two different trails."

"Or they could be hidden somewhere, staying quiet and out of sight until we're all gone." Jo tapped a finger against her chin.

After that, the five of us sat in silence, but it wasn't the comfortable kind. We were all aware that the archer might still be nearby, and even if none of us had been the target, there was still a feeling of danger in the air. All of us, except Wyatt, jumped at the sound of voices about twenty minutes later.

Five constables soon sprinted into view, and Jo immediately called out to Gordon, telling him to let them inspect the arrow. He waddled over to his witch with Perkins still on his back. Even Wyatt smiled to see my burrowing owl riding the pelican like a horse.

One of the constables had carried a bag full of tools for collecting evidence, and soon, there was a lot of measuring and photo-taking happening. Wyatt gave his team a rundown of the incident, and I heard someone say that witnesses had been asked to go to the tavern to give their accounts. "It seemed like a safer option than the parking lot, considering the circumstances," the constable concluded.

Sit a Spell Tavern seemed like an odd choice to me, and I said so to Valerian, but she shrugged. "It's got plenty of space for witnesses to hang out, and there's nowhere in there an archer could hide."

"You should be there, making calming potions for everyone," Jo said.

Valerian looked thoughtful. "I wonder if people tip better after a traumatic event?"

It was another twenty minutes before Marlee announced she was feeling well enough to head back to the parking lot. When the rest of us protested, she said, "The walk will be good for me. Just us and our familiars, and none of these extra emotions." She waved in the direction of the constables.

Before we started the long walk, I let Wyatt know where we were going.

"You'll need to head to the tavern, like everyone else," he said. "One of the constables there will take your statement."

That would make Valerian happy. She could help solve a crime and rake in tips at the same time.

"Be careful," I told Wyatt.

"You, too. I want you ladies to be vigilant and keep your familiars on guard."

We were, perhaps, a little too vigilant on our walk to the parking lot. For the first half hour, we would all jump and let out a little squeak every time an owl hooted or a branch snapped. I had to stop three times to shed all the excess magic I was building up.

Perkins had returned to his perch on my shoulder, but the other three birds flew over our heads. Gordon was swooping back and forth, like he was on patrol, while Stella flew slightly ahead of us. Lonnie brought up the rear, fluttering from one low branch to another.

Eventually, we all calmed down enough that Marlee commented on it. She declared she was still exhausted but feeling a lot more centered.

When we reached the parking lot, I saw the expected Foxfire Haven Constables sedans, but there were about five other vehicles, as well.

"Those must belong to the people who ran the wrong direction down the trail," Valerian commented. "Do you think any of them have figured it out yet?"

"The way people were panicking, they might not stop until they reach Oregon." Marlee yawned, then added, "I'm going to need help at the tavern."

"Like a shielding spell?" Jo asked. "We've done that for you before, and we can do it again."

We all agreed to do a shielding spell before walking inside the tavern, and we'd keep a close eye on Marlee to make sure the people gathered there weren't causing any further problems for her.

I had known Sit a Spell would be crowded, but I was still surprised at just how packed the place was. Every seat was occupied. People had settled onto the wooden floor along two of the walls, and more were standing around.

"Where are the constables?" I asked as we picked our way through the crowd.

Jo pointed. "There, behind the bar." Sure enough, three constables were standing to one side, each taking statements from a witness. One of those witnesses, I noticed, was Adeline.

"That's where I'm going," Valerian said. "I'll start making calming potions as fast as I can. It will help all these people settle down, which will protect Marlee."

"Can we do anything?" I asked.

Valerian thought for a moment. "Yes. If each of us is measuring out ingredients, it will go faster. But, Marlee, you're not helping. You're going to go sit in Will's office. If he's in there, you tell him that desk chair belongs to you for the rest of the night."

"If he doesn't surrender the chair to me, I'll threaten him with a tornado," Marlee promised.

Our familiars found space on the shelves to sit, so the four of them watched over us as Valerian began giving instructions to Jo and me. In short order, we had an efficient assembly line going, and another bartender began to deliver the drinks to tables.

"At least it feels safe here," I commented as I carefully tipped a glass jar full of dried chamomile flowers into a measuring cup.

Jo was mincing dill, and she paused to joke, "Maybe we need your stalker, Val. He's been so desperate to keep you safe from these hunters, but now that there's real trouble, he's nowhere to be found."

Adeline must have finished giving her statement, because she walked away from the constable she'd been talking to. Before making her way out from behind the bar, she stopped and leaned forward, so her head was between Jo's and mine.

"Hazel," Adeline said, "I hope you catch Vincent's killer soon. I have a feeling his death and tonight's attack are related."

"I agree, but you should be saying you hope the constables catch the killer soon, not me."

Adeline laughed quietly. "I guess I should have said that I hope the killer is caught soon. I don't really care who does the catching."

I heard a muffled sob, followed by a hiccup. On the other side of the bar, Natalie had squeezed her way between two people sitting on stools. Her mascara had left black smudges under her eyes, which were puffy from crying. As I watched, she hitched in a rattling breath, then hiccupped again.

Behind Natalie, one of the women in her coven gripped her shoulder, but I couldn't tell if it was in sympathy or in warning. "Watch what you say, Nat," the woman said.

"I have to tell her," Natalie insisted. She sniffed, wiped at her eyes, then gave Adeline a pleading look. "I wanted you to be miserable, but I never really wanted you to die. And now, you're going to, and it's all my fault!"

Chapter Twenty-Four

Adeline stepped forward and braced her arms on the bar while Jo and I scrambled to get away from the confrontation. "What do you mean, I'm going to die?" she asked Natalie.

Jo leaned toward me. In a low whisper, she asked, "Wasn't Shawna yelling at Adeline just an hour or two ago?"

I'm not even sure I nodded my head. I was too absorbed in the scene before me to think about anything else.

It took a bit before Natalie could answer Adeline's question, because she had started crying again. Her sobs were so loud most of the bar had fallen silent. Even Valerian, I noticed, had given up making potions so she could watch what was unfolding.

"I haven't been hiding the fact that my coven and I did a karma spell against you," Natalie finally said. Except, her voice was so thick from crying it was difficult to understand her. "My coven" sounded more like "by cubbin."

"Yes, I know." Adeline leaned over the bar menacingly. "You've been telling this whole town, so of course word got around to me."

"Well, what I didn't tell you is that it's not the only spell I did." Again, the woman holding Natalie's shoulder gave her a warning squeeze. This time, she made a shushing noise. "No, Denise, I need to say this. I can't carry around this guilt!"

Denise let go of Natalie's shoulder and stepped back. Her tone was icy as she spat, "Suit yourself."

I knew that Marlee, Jo, and Valerian would never abandon me when I was trying to get through such a difficult situation. For the first time since I'd met her, I felt a wave of sympathy for Natalie.

That sympathy disappeared when she blurted, "I worked dark magic against you! I'm so sorry, Adeline, but I did a spell that you'd be pierced through the heart with remorse. I wanted you to suffer, but I didn't want you to die! That arrow tonight, it was meant for you, I'm sure, and you would have literally been pierced through the heart."

I firmly told myself that I was not going to get involved in the conversation, but my curiosity quickly won out over sense. "How do you know the archer was trying to hit Adeline?"

Natalie ran her fingers through her hair, which was tangled and frizzy. She had probably been making that motion for a while. "The arrowhead was silver-coated wood. It was designed to kill either a shifter or a vampire."

Silver to the heart was the way to kill a werewolf or any other kind of shifter, and the wooden arrowhead essentially turned the arrow into a wooden stake. But Natalie hadn't given me a satisfactory answer. "Maybe the archer was aiming for a shifter," I pointed out.

"No, it was Adeline. I'm sure of it." Natalie held her hands out, palms up, as if she were holding the arrow. "It had her name painted on the shaft. The arrow was spelled against her."

The Adeline I knew was a strong woman who wasn't easily unnerved. But, as she processed what Natalie was saying, she swayed slightly and passed a hand over her eyes. Jo reached out, ready to catch her if she fainted.

"How, exactly, do you know this?" Valerian asked. She sounded like she believed Natalie's story as much as the rumor about hunters being in town.

"The constables told me." Natalie jerked a thumb over her shoulder. "There were two of them talking outside, and I heard one of them say the team in the woods saw the name on the arrow."

I resisted the temptation to point out that Natalie hadn't been told anything. She'd simply overheard a conversation that had definitely not been meant for her ears. And, now, the entire tavern would know.

Wyatt was not going to be happy about that.

Adeline turned to me. "I still don't think there are any hunters," she said.

"My coven and I were discussing it, and we agreed that someone wants to perpetuate the rumor," I told her.

"But why? And why are they targeting me?" Adeline shook her head. "I get that some people believe I killed Vincent, but who could have liked him enough to want to get vigilante justice? Who in this town is willing to kill me because of him?"

I didn't have an answer to that. I also wasn't sure that was why Adeline's name had been on the arrow. Maybe it had been done to scare her.

Or, I considered, maybe Adeline had set up the whole thing to make herself look more innocent.

That seemed unlikely, but I told myself not to discount any of the theories. Sometimes, the weirdest answer turned out to be the right answer.

"Ms. Beaumont," broke in one of the constables, "I think we need to take you into protective custody. We've got a subterranean cell for vampires you can stay in."

Adeline grimaced. "I am not going to sleep in a jail cell! If you want to keep me safe, send a couple of constables to my house before dawn."

The constable looked like he wanted to argue, but when Adeline bared her teeth just enough for her fangs to show, he said, "As long as the chief constable approves of that plan."

"In the meantime, I'm going to my magic store. I'll be safe enough there."

"Vincent wasn't," quipped a woman standing nearby.

Adeline vaulted over the bar and landed in front of the woman in one smooth motion, moving so fast she was just a blur. The woman wisely ducked her head, turned around, and hustled away.

"I'll let you know if I hear anything helpful," I promised Adeline, hoping to placate her at least a little.

"Thank you, Hazel. I appreciate you believing in me."

Adeline didn't have to weave through the crowd to get to the door. People stepped back and cleared a wide path for her, clearly terrified of her wrath.

"Maybe this was the point," Jo said. When Valerian and I turned to her, she explained, "If someone is dead set on framing Adeline for Vincent's death, doing things to bring out her temper is a good way of making her look guilty. It's not often any of us sees a vampire move at their predatory speed, or leap over a bar like it was an anthill."

"You think someone wants to provoke Adeline. It's a good theory." Valerian turned to the constable. "How many more witnesses need to give their statements?"

"About a dozen more, plus you and your coven."

"We'll keep making the calming potions until you're ready to talk to us."

The constable nodded grimly. "I think that's a wise idea."

The rest of the evening was comparatively quiet. The whole tavern had started buzzing as soon as Adeline left, and quite a few people stuck around long after giving their statements, but there were no more confrontations.

It was eleven o'clock by the time I was pulled into a corner to give my statement. It took much longer than it should have for me to tell my version of the night's events, because I was yawning so often. Eventually, it was done, and Will told Valerian to grab her coven, head home, and get some rest.

All of us were happy to comply, except Marlee. We found her in Will's office, fast asleep in his desk chair. We hated having to rouse her, but we knew Marlee would rather be in her own bed. After we woke her up, Marlee agreed with that logic, though she did grumble about being ripped out of a dream about having a romantic picnic lunch with Garth.

"Sounds like a good date once the weather warms up a bit," I told her.

On our way out of the tavern, I saw that Natalie and her coven were still sitting in one of the booths. I was surprised to realize there didn't seem to be any hard feelings for the woman who had left Natalie alone to confess her dark magic to Adeline.

I had hoped we would just pass by their booth without incident, but Natalie called my name. I braced myself for another emotional outburst, then turned to face her.

"You're friends with Adeline, right?" Natalie asked.

"I wouldn't say that."

"But you're helping her. I saw you two talking. Will you please tell her that I'm suffering the consequences of my actions? The remorse I wanted her to feel has rebounded on me." Natalie pressed a hand against her heart.

As gently as I could, I said, "I think Adeline would appreciate hearing that from you. However, maybe you should wait a bit, until we're past all of this."

Shawna appeared at my elbow. While everyone else in the tavern looked scared and emotionally drained, she looked bright and excited. "I have a pre-packaged spell for bravery, Natalie. Or, if you prefer a non-confrontational solution, you can use one of my pre-written apology incantations. It helps the person you've hurt know you want forgiveness, but you don't have to say a word to them."

"Sounds like you've got a lot of options, Natalie," I said. "Good night."

Before Shawna could try to sell me some kind of magic I didn't need, I rejoined my coven, and we drove home.

That night, I had nightmares about being lost in the woods with Natalie, who wailed every time we heard an owl hoot.

I was still hearing hooting when I opened my eyes the next morning, but at least I was no longer hearing Natalie crying hysterically.

It was Perkins who was calling to me while he hopped up and down on my pillow.

"Okay, okay," I mumbled. "I'm up."

Perkins gave another hop, and the pillow bobbed under my head. That got me to sit up, and I looked at the clock to see I'd slept through my alarm. Thankfully, I hadn't overslept that much, because I had a delivery to make that morning. I could still have a long, hot shower and enjoy my morning coffee before I had to leave the house.

Jo was already sitting at the table when I shuffled into the kitchen. She had one hand curled around a steaming mug of coffee, and the other was holding her cell phone to her ear. From her side of the conversation, I knew she was discussing a story with her editor.

I slid into a chair across from Jo just as she hung up, and she blew out a breath. "Sam has asked me to write the story about what happened during the search party last night. Being an eyewitness to so much drama does have its benefits."

I groaned in answer.

"Why am I awake so early?" Valerian asked. She was standing in the doorway, and she had wrapped herself in a fuzzy blanket. Its red-and-green-plaid design clashed with her orange-and-purple flannel pajamas.

"Did you also have nightmares?" I asked.

"Surprisingly, no. I did, however, wake up with wrist pain. I think I made too many potions last night!" Valerian joined us at the table after getting her own cup of coffee. Marlee, I was sure, was still asleep.

The three of us sipped our coffee quietly. I was still trying to wake up properly, and there just didn't seem to be much to say about the search party. We'd already discussed it with each other and told the constables everything we'd witnessed, and still, we had so many questions.

When the doorbell rang, we all jumped. Valerian and I both spilled coffee onto the table.

Jo let out a shaky laugh. "That scared me!"

"I'll get it," I offered. Jo was writing down notes for her newspaper article, and Valerian was still bundled in the blanket.

It was only nine o'clock in the morning, and I wondered what had brought Wyatt to our door. Because, I was sure, it was him. Either he was checking on Marlee or he had something about the case he wanted to discuss.

I opened the door wide. "Good morning, Wy—"

I didn't even have time to register what was happening. There was a blur of movement in front of me, then my whole body was shoved sideways, into the wall. I heard heavy footsteps running down the hall, toward the back of the house, and a deafening wail that sounded like it had come right out of my nightmare.

Chapter Twenty-Five

I PRESSED MY HANDS over my ears as I sagged against the doorframe. The poltergeist was responsible for the wailing, I knew, and even though the sound was painful, I was grateful that it would warn Valerian and Jo that something was wrong.

The person who had run past me reached the end of the main hallway and paused, looking left and right. It was only then I saw their face.

"Harris!" I said with a gasp. As I watched, he turned right into the back hallway, heading straight for the kitchen.

My heart felt like it was going to pound right out of my chest, and I had one clear thought: *Call Wyatt.* I reached for my phone in the back pocket of my jeans, but it wasn't there. I had left it sitting on my nightstand.

The nearest phone was Marlee's, since her bedroom was at the front of the house. I banged on her door and shouted her name, and Marlee opened it almost immediately. She was still tying her bathrobe around her waist. "What's going on?" she shouted over the poltergeist's din.

“Harris just pushed past me and is running for the kitchen! Val and Jo are in there!”

Marlee swiftly moved past me, in the direction of the kitchen, but I caught her arm. “I need your phone to call Wyatt,” I told her.

She turned to retrieve it from her bedroom, but before she could do so, the door slammed shut. Marlee tried to turn the knob, then pushed against the door with her shoulder. It didn’t budge. “Poltergeist, I need to get inside!”

Instead of complying, there were several loud knocks on the wall next to the door. They were followed by a few more knocks a bit farther down the hallway, then another knock beyond that.

“I think it wants us to go to the kitchen,” I said. I shook my hands, and pink sparks flew from my fingertips. I had to shed my magic before I made the situation worse. “It’s trying to get us to follow the knocking.”

Marlee grabbed my hand, and the two of us hustled to the kitchen while I mouthed the words for my shedding spell. As we ran, I heard a loud thud, squawking, and a shout of distress.

When we reached the kitchen, I stopped just inside the doorway and snorted out a laugh. Harris was the one in danger rather than anyone in my coven. He was sprawled on his back on the floor, and Gordon was standing on his chest, nipping at Harris’s nose with the tip of his beak. Lonnie was perched on Harris’s forehead, her curved raven’s beak dangerously close to one of his eyes.

Stella had one of Harris's fingers gripped in her beak, and Perkins was standing next to his head, hooting into his ear loudly.

"Ow!" Harris swatted at Gordon with his free hand, but the pelican didn't budge. "Let me go, you stupid birds! I'm trying to help!"

"Then why did you run in here like you were going to attack us?" Jo asked. She and Valerian had both risen from their chairs, and a coffee cup was on its side, its contents slowly dripping from the table onto the floor.

"I was worried after I heard the news."

"What news?" Valerian asked sharply.

Harris said something, but it was drowned out by the poltergeist's continued wailing.

I lifted my head toward the ceiling. "Please stop!" I yelled. "Thank you for your help, but we have this under control now!"

The wailing ceased immediately.

"At least it knows how to follow instructions," Marlee commented.

Perkins stopped trilling into Harris's ear and looked at me with his head tilted sideways.

"You can quiet down, too," I told him, "but be ready, just in case."

Marlee told Stella to let go of Harris's finger, and Lonnie reluctantly hopped off his forehead.

At a word from Jo, Gordon stayed put but ceased his nipping at Harris's nose.

"Can I at least sit up?" Harris asked, eyeing Gordon warily.

"Not yet," Jo said. "Now, tell us this news that has you so upset."

"The news about what happened during the search in the woods last night." Harris said it like it should have been obvious. "Everyone in town is talking about the arrow that flew through the crowd."

Valerian scoffed. "So, what, you came here to guard us, in case the archer knocks on the door?"

"Obviously. I know you four were there last night. Valerian, you were in danger as much as Adeline was. You nearly got taken out by that arrow."

I rubbed my right elbow. "I think you might have bruised me on your way inside just now. If you're trying to protect us, you're not doing a very good job of it."

There were soft footsteps in the hallway, followed by a light tapping against the doorframe. We turned to see Shawna standing there, her eyes wide as she looked from Harris to the rest of us.

"Your front door was wide open," Shawna said. "I worried something was wrong, so I came on in."

"Harris barged past me, and I forgot to close the door," I explained.

"I'm trying to help!" Harris said defensively.

Shawna laughed. "He beat me to it."

"To what?" Valerian asked. "Nearly giving us all a heart attack?"

"The opposite, in fact. I came here to help, too, by giving you peace of mind." Shawna reached into a canvas tote bag that dangled from one shoulder and pulled out a handful of small indigo-colored bags. They were all filled with something that gave off a faint sweet scent. "These charm bags are my most popular item. I call it Boundary in a Bag. Wear it around your neck, put it on your nightstand, carry it in your purse: use it wherever you need a protective barrier to feel safe. I thought, after last night, you ladies could each use one of these."

"How much?" Valerian asked skeptically.

"Free for the four of you."

I was about to ask what the catch was, since Shawna seemed like a determined saleswoman, but she answered my question before I could ask it. "Consider it a gesture of goodwill. I didn't kill Vincent, even though Adeline thinks I did."

Shawna knew Adeline had asked for my help in clearing her name, and she was hoping to butter me up with a bit of free magic.

Marlee laughed suddenly. "You said Harris beat you to it, but he did not bring us peace of mind."

"I was trying to," he muttered. "I've got spelled coins for safety, and I was going to give one to each of you."

"He bought them from me early this morning. The coins aren't as powerful as my bags," Shawna said, "but they are easy to carry in a pocket."

What a ridiculous situation, I thought. We were standing in our kitchen, looking at a man pinned to the ground by a pelican while getting a sales pitch from a less-than-scrupulous entrepreneurial witch.

When I heard Holman's voice from the hallway, I knew things were about to get even more bizarre. "Right this way." His tone was polite, but I heard an undercurrent of fear. I hadn't known it was possible to scare a ghost.

Holman drifted through the kitchen doorway with Wyatt on his heels.

"What are you doing here?" I blurted. "I wanted to call you, but I couldn't."

"Holman did it for you."

Shawna was blinking at the ghost as if she didn't believe her own eyes. Valerian, Jo, Marlee, and I were all gaping at him, too, but for a completely different reason.

"Holman, you made a phone call?" Jo asked breathlessly.

"I've never used one of those fancy cordless pocket-phones," Holman said proudly, "but I've watched all of you do it enough that I knew how. I went into Hazel's room and called the chief constable."

"But my phone requires entering a six-digit passcode," I pointed out.

Holman rolled his eyes. "I've seen you enter it a thousand times. It took me a while to touch all the numbers, but I managed to do it."

"Thank you, Holman," I said. The rest of my coven echoed their gratitude.

"Would someone please explain why a ghost called me here?" Wyatt asked. "Also, why is Mr. Kneale on the floor?"

Everyone began talking at once, and Wyatt raised his arms and made a patting motion. Once we quieted down, he looked at me. "I would love a cup of coffee while I deal with whatever is going on here."

"Coming right up." I edged past Harris and Shawna to retrieve a cup. As I grabbed a coffee mug from the cabinet, my eyes fell on a delicate teacup next to it. I thought suddenly of the incident at Stacy's Stationery and Sundries. I had felt so guilty for exploding all those teacups, but I wasn't the one who had started the chain reaction that led to that.

Ultimately, the blame for the teacups fell on the maker's girlfriend, who had cursed them in the first place. If she hadn't been angry enough to curse her boyfriend, then nothing else would have happened.

Slowly, I pulled the teacup out of the cupboard and turned it thoughtfully in my fingers. "Petty revenge," I muttered.

"Hazel?" Wyatt prompted.

I shook my head. I had an idea that was forming, but I wasn't quite there yet. Some piece of the puzzle was still missing. Instead, I replaced the teacup and retrieved the coffee mug. When I handed Wyatt his coffee, though, I realized my hands were shaking.

"Shawna, I thought you might have started the rumor about hunters being in the area," I said. "I thought you were doing it to get more business, because you knew people would be clamoring for protection and shielding magic."

"I didn't start a rumor," Shawna said hotly. "People have seen hunters in town."

"Have they? Has anyone really confirmed that? Because, now, I think Natalie Gil started that rumor to get under Adeline's skin."

"You think she wasn't content with working dark magic against her," Valerian guessed. "She wanted to scare Adeline, too, so she made up the rumor."

"I think that's exactly what happened. But I think it got out of hand and went far beyond what Natalie had intended. She never meant to create a town-wide panic, and she never thought there would be a search party for the hunters. I think that's the real reason she was crying last night. She didn't feel remorse about working magic against Adeline. She was remorseful about starting a rumor that spiraled out of control."

"But you all saw her last night," Shawna broke in. "She was as scared as the rest of us when that arrow hit the tree."

"Maybe she was worried that her lie had become a truth," Marlee said.

"It's possible she thought she had manifested a hunter's arrival by accident and felt guilty," Jo agreed. She sounded more sympathetic than angry, and I knew she was thinking of her own unexpected outcomes with magical manifesting.

"Or," I said, "she realized someone was using the rumor to stir up panic, someone only pretending to be a hunter last night."

Someone who wasn't in the crowd of people. Someone who hadn't cared enough to support the town, or the organizer of the search.

Or, maybe, they had cared a lot.

Finally, the idea that had been forming in my mind clicked into place. "And by someone, I mean Harris. He's the one who shot the arrow."

Harris sat up so quickly he sent Gordon flying off his chest and into the air. "Why would I do something like that?"

"So everyone would believe a hunter had killed Vincent. You even wrote Adeline's name on the arrow, so it would look like a hunter was targeting her, too. You hoped that, in time, everyone would accept that a hunter was behind both attacks, and the case would be closed, because you didn't want anyone learning that you're the one who staked Vincent."

Shawna made a high-pitched noise that wasn't so different from the poltergeist's wails. "That can't be true."

Harris stood up, then stalked toward me. Wyatt halted his forward motion with a hand against his chest. "Look," Harris said hotly, "I know my feelings for Val are a bit intense, but I didn't kill Vincent just because he was flirting with her."

"No, you killed him because he was taking business away from your best friend, Connor."

Harris stepped back, and I saw his eyes dart around the room. "He was mesmerizing Connor's clients, too. Did you know that? He was using his stupid vampire power to steal Connor's clients, and he was using dark magic to amplify it. Connor was trying to work reciprocal spells, but Vincent was stronger. When I saw him walk into the magic store, I knew he was going to buy things to do more magic against Connor, so I found an old board in the alley and broke it to give it a sharp end. The back door was unlocked, so I snuck in, saw the fuse box, and flipped the switch to turn off the security—"

Harris stopped and clapped a hand over his mouth, as if only just noticing his denial had turned into a confession.

"Well done, Hazel," Wyatt said. "Now, if you ladies—and you, Holman—will all excuse me, I have an arrest to make."

As soon as Wyatt had left the kitchen, a handcuffed Harris walking dejectedly in front of him, Shawna turned to me. "I have a great spell kit for clearing all the negative energy Harris just dumped in your kitchen. I'll even give you ladies a bulk discount."

Chapter Twenty-Six

"I STILL CAN'T BELIEVE you figured out who staked Vincent because you saw a teacup in our cupboard," Valerian said.

It had been two days since Wyatt had arrested Harris, and my friends were still eagerly discussing what we had started referring to as our kitchen adventure. All four of us were sitting at the table, sipping our morning coffee while our familiars looked on.

"I thought about the teacup maker's girlfriend cursing the cups," I explained for what must have been the tenth time. Not that I was getting tired of telling the story. I'd repeated it for my coven a few times, Jo had demanded to know every detail of my thought process for her newspaper story, and I'd had to give a statement to the constables.

Plus, there were my clients. My deliveries the day before had taken twice as long as usual because each client wanted a blow-by-blow account.

"I get that's how you realized Natalie started the rumor," Marlee said. She had recovered from her empathic overwhelm and was looking much perkier. "In both cases, one small mean act against an individual blew up—"

"Literally, for the teacups," Jo interjected.

"Yes, and many people who were wholly uninvolved in the drama got caught up in it." Marlee shook her head. "At least this town has gone back to normal."

"Wyatt says he got another call yesterday about hunters in the area," I said, "but for the most part, people have realized it was all just an out-of-control lie."

"Hopefully, Shawna enjoyed the boost in business while she had it." Valerian shook her head. "She's probably making a pre-mixed Recover from the Rumors potion."

"If she's not," Jo said, "then you should. I bet you could sell a lot of those at the tavern."

"Before I start concocting a new potion, back to Hazel figuring out Harris was the killer. I'm still astounded that you made the connection between him and Connor."

I waved a hand. "I should have realized it when the two of them were in the tavern together. Like we discussed that night at The Salt Circle when the hunter rumors were swirling, the simplest solution is the most likely. Connor was being hurt by Vincent, so Connor's best friend took Vincent out."

Jo nodded. "The hunter rumor Natalie started, and even Adeline's feuds with both Shawna and Natalie, were totally unrelated drama."

"Harris knew the arrow had passed close to Valerian," I continued. "However, that incident happened after the werewolf brothers escorted Harris away from the search party. I realized he must have seen the arrow sail past Val, and I figured that meant he had snuck back and shot the arrow himself."

"Which was probably his plan from the start." Valerian's face twisted. "He was flirting with me more than usual that night, and I think he wanted to get kicked out of the group. He doubted anyone would suspect him of coming back to shoot an arrow into the crowd, and everyone would panic that a hunter was after us."

"All to make himself look innocent." I looked around at my friends. "I know you all have my back, but please don't go out and stake a vampire on my behalf."

"You do not need to worry about that," Marlee assured me. "What we need to be worrying about is this energy vortex. I'm glad to know the poltergeist seems to be on our side, but between its growing power and our magic expanding to uncontrollable levels, we have to find a solution soon."

"I found two spells that might help curb the energy here," I said.

Valerian nodded. "Plus, I'm working on a potion that will make us immune to it. Or, at any rate, we won't absorb as much of it. A sort of energy-blocker potion."

"I'd say I could write an intention, but the way those have been going lately..." Jo didn't need to dive into the what-ifs.

"I only have one delivery this afternoon, so I'll keep researching solutions," I promised. "But, right now, I need to go get ready."

"For your date with your boyfriend!" Marlee was grinning.

"It is not a date, and he is not my boyfriend."

Wyatt had, though, asked me to join him for breakfast at The Salt Circle. After taking Harris to the station and dealing with closing out the case of Vincent's staking,

Wyatt had stopped by the funeral home to check on all of us. We'd assured him we were fine, though we had barely escaped getting Shawna out the door without us agreeing to buy anything from her.

Then, quite unexpectedly, Wyatt had asked me to meet him for breakfast in a couple of days. He had seemed as shocked by the invitation as I was, but I had agreed. Even though I was having a tough time controlling my magic when I was around Wyatt, we were, at least, getting along better.

So, at two minutes before ten, I walked into The Salt Circle, feeling rather nervous but also grateful that Wyatt no longer held the title of Grumpiest Man in Foxfire Haven.

Wyatt was already there, seated at a booth with his hands curled around a mug of coffee.

"Good morning," I said as I slid onto the bench opposite him.

"It is a good morning. A nice, sunny, crime-free morning."

"How is Harris adjusting to his new living quarters?"

Wyatt grimaced. "The jail is only temporary. After his trial, he'll be moved to the prison in Vesta Falls. He keeps trying to convince the guards that Vincent deserved to be staked, and that his loss is Foxfire Haven's gain."

"At least Val no longer has to deal with his obsession over her," I said. I suppressed a shudder. "He always gave me the creeps, but I thought it was because of the way he leered at Val."

A server came over with a fresh cup of coffee for me. Since I'd already had two cups at home that morning, I knew I would be practically vibrating from the caffeine after having another cup. As I sipped slowly, Wyatt and I made small talk until we'd put in our order for breakfast. Then, he shifted his weight and leaned over the table.

"Thank you, Hazel."

"You know I'm happy to help solve a murder, especially when it involves people I know." People like Adeline, who had been downright friendly to me the night before, when I'd gone into the magic store. Maybe things between her and me were going to be okay in the future.

"I'm not talking about you figuring out who killed Vincent, though I am grateful for that." Wyatt hesitated, and he began absently picking at his napkin with his fingers. "I'm saying thank you because you, well, you didn't judge me when I told you I'd lost my magic."

"I understand how grief can have an impact on every facet of our lives." Suddenly, I leaned forward, too, and put a hand over one of Wyatt's. "What if the energy vortex could help you get your magic back? You said the dead started talking to you of their own accord there, so we know you're affected by whatever is happening at the funeral home."

"I'm not sure it's going to be that easy, but maybe it's worth a shot." Wyatt's serious expression turned teasing, and his blue eyes sparkled. "I should start hanging out there, especially around dinnertime."

"You're always welcome with us," I assured him.

"As long as you promise not to have a magical exhalation and send stew flying through the kitchen."

"I have too much magic, and you don't have enough," I said, laughing. I squeezed Wyatt's hand. "Don't worry. We'll find our balance."

A NOTE FROM THE AUTHOR

Thank you for coming along on another magical adventure with my Crones of a Feather! If you want to explore my other cozy, spooky worlds, did you know that you can try each one with a free short story? When you sign up for my newsletter, you'll get instant access to them.

You can start with *Chaos at the Coffee Shop*, a fun standalone story in my Nightmare, Arizona world starring Felipe the chupacabra! If you prefer ghosts, you might enjoy *Quality Service*, a prequel to my Eternal Rest Bed and Breakfast series.

You can find the links on my website under "Reading Order." Happy reading!

Eternally Yours,

Beth

P.S. You can find paperbacks, reading order, merch, and more at BethDolgner.com!

Next in Series

Find out what's next for Hazel and the Crones of a Feather!

Familiars and Foul Play
Crones of a Feather Paranormal Cozy Mysteries Book 5

An unrepentant bride, a magical murder, and a Bigfoot in hiding. The outside world has its eye on the witches of Foxfire Haven.

When Hazel Underwood and her coven of middle-aged witches stumble on a dead body in the woods, it sure looks like the work of dark magic. Unfortunately, the case falls under the jurisdiction of a non-magical town, and the sheriff there is looking at the witches a little too closely.

Meanwhile, the coven has to protect the town's resident Bigfoot, Barry, when a Bigfoot hunter rolls into town. Is it a coincidence that the hunter has ties to the murder victim?

While the residents of Foxfire Haven struggle to protect their magical secrets from being discovered, Hazel also has to deal with the growing energy vortex inside her home. As the energy grows, more and more witches' familiars are being drawn into the chaos...

AMAZON

US | UK | CA | AU | DE

ACKNOWLEDGMENTS

Thank you, as always, to my amazing readers who are part of my production team: my test readers and ARC readers. All of you make such a big difference, and I appreciate you! Thanks to Lia at Your Best Book Editor for another great round of copy editing, and an extra-special thank you to Kelly at Partners in Crime Book Services for jumping in at the last minute to proofread for me.

And, to all of you who enjoy getting lost in these worlds along with me, thank you. Because you read my books, I get to keep writing them.

BOOKS BY BETH DOLGNER

Crones of a Feather
Paranormal Cozy Mystery Series
Spells and Subterfuge
Divination and Deceit
Manifesting and Mischief
Crystals and Conspiracies
Familiars and Foul Play

Nightmare, Arizona
Paranormal Cozy Mystery Series
Homicide at the Haunted House
Drowning at the Diner
Slaying at the Saloon
Murder at the Motel
Poisoning at the Party
Headless at Halloween (Novella)
Clawing at the Corral
Axing at the Antique Store
Fatality at the Festival
Terminated at the Trailhead
Body at the Bakery

Eternal Rest Bed and Breakfast

Paranormal Cozy Mystery Series

Sweet Dreams
Late Checkout
Picture Perfect
Destination Wedding (Novella)
Scenic Views
Breakfast Included
Groups Welcome
Quiet Nights
Halloween Vibes (Novella)

Betty Boo, Ghost Hunter

Romantic Urban Fantasy Series

Ghost of a Threat
Ghost of a Whisper
Ghost of a Memory
Ghost of a Hope

Manifest

Young Adult Steampunk

A Talent for Death

Young Adult Urban Fantasy

Non-fiction

Georgia Spirits and Specters
Everyday Voodoo

ABOUT THE AUTHOR

Beth Dolgner's career as an author began in nonfiction with *Georgia Spirits and Specters*, a collection of Georgia ghost stories. From there, Beth entered the world of ghost hunting and was a longtime guide with the Roswell Ghost Tour in Georgia. She also lectures on Victorian death and mourning customs as well as Victorian Spiritualism, which stemmed from her volunteer work with Atlanta's Historic Oakland Cemetery. Beth likes to think of it all as research for her books.

Outside of writing, Beth enjoys traveling, sewing, and trying to convince her husband, Ed, that ghosts are real.

Keep up with Beth and sign up for her newsletter at BethDolgner.com.

www.ingramcontent.com/pod-product-compliance
Lightning Source LLC
LaVergne TN
LVHW091134080826
845145LV00008B/2145